Note from the author

AF209929

This novel can be read in three different ways:

1) as it was printed;
2) following first Arabic numerals (including Prologue and Epilogue) and then Roman numerals; or
3) following first Roman numerals and then Arabic numerals (including Prologue and Epilogue).

Whichever option you go for, I guarantee you will not feel lost at any point. I could suggest a way of reading this book, but I do not want to bias you in any way. If you acquired a physical copy and decide to read it as indicated on numbers 2 or 3, you might want to add a bookmark to the 'Index of chapters' page, as you will be coming back quite a lot.

I sincerely hope you have a good time reading my debut novel.

All the best,

Giovanna.

© 2022, Giovanna de la Hoz
Printed and published by: BoD - Books on
Demand, Norderstedt
ISBN: 9788413735542

Index of Chapters

Prologue

The suffocating heat they had been experiencing since the beginning of the summer was something she had not experienced ever before. She was by herself in a now-not-so-unknown, yet excitingly new city, and on her last day of work before the summer holidays, she was pondering the options that her first holidays as a young working adult offered her. She had just moved into her new place, where she was to live for what was remaining of her contract. Or so she hoped.

Even though her previous housemate had been a nice and easy-going girl, they had not gotten along more than what had been extremely necessary. Despite how awkward their encounters within the small apartment had been however, they had always been kindly friendly to each other. Yet that had been it.

Determined to live a much pleasant experience with her new housemate, she had moved in a couple of days earlier than what they had first agreed on. Unfortunately for her, her first night at her new place had not felt as welcoming as she had dreamed it would be. Besides having gotten her period that very same morning, which was a circumstance that was annoying enough on its own, the extreme heat they had been experiencing for the last weeks had made sleeping a real struggle. A struggle that was twice as annoying when one had to get up early to go to work. Nonetheless, she had gotten up that morning hoping for the last-day-in-the-office mood to help ease that pain to smoothly get her along the day.

She had had to relocate to her current location because of work. She had been all in since she had gotten the job offer. That much in fact, that the excitement of the transition from being a university student to becoming a young working adult had gotten her blind to the need she had of her family. She had not spent a single day without having a thought for everyone she had left behind, yet she had so often found herself amid such a fast-moving reality, that she had sometimes forgotten to phone her loved ones. Thus, as soon as she got home from work that day, she took out her mobile phone and dialled her grandfather.

'Grandpa!' shouted Eileen, relieved when her grandfather finally answered the phone. Even though he was nimble enough for his age (some youngsters wished they were as agile as he was), he had probably been working at his vegetable garden, and thus it had taken him longer to answer the phone. The waiting for Eileen had been tedious, but luckily for her, it was over now. 'Thank Goodness you answered! I was starting to worry. You alright?'.

'Sure I am, Eileen. Why wouldn' I?'.

'Nothing... Just forget about it. The heat might have gotten me more sensitive,' said Eileen, trying to downplay her concern. She had always had a special connection with her grandfather, and the sole thought of him having any problem made her worry in excess. 'Anyway, long story short... we got home earlier from work today, so I'll be able to head off to Pitlochry this evening! I might as well just take a nap before though, I didn't get much sleep last night. So... yeah, I guess I could be home for a late dinner. How do you like that?'.

'Fer real? That's awesome!' said Alick. He had decided to let Eileen's first comment go on purpose, and just focus on how excited the news had gotten him. 'Yer grandma is going to love it when I tell her. Lemme just finish up wate'ing the plants, and I'll let her know. But please, don' hurry. Mind yerself on the road!'.

'That I will, grandpa,' said Eileen, restraining to let the tears that had suddenly come to her eyes roll all over her face. If only he knew how excited she was to finally visit them… 'I was originally coming tomorrow, but I've realised that what I have left to do here can be done when I return after the holidays. Also, you know what we say, don't you?'.

'Family fi'st,' was all Alick said for a reply.

'Always,' said Eileen while letting two emotional tears plough through her face. She wiped them away with the back of her hand and remained expectant to whatever her grandfather might add. But neither of them was able to speak without emotionally cracking, so gathering all her strength, Eileen added: 'see you later, grandpa'.

She had tried for her voice not to tremble, but she could not be sure she had managed that. Her grandfather had always seemed to have a sixth sense regarding her, so she had since long learned that there were no hiding secrets from him. As determined as she was to kick start her holidays the best way possible however, she set an alarm on her phone and got herself ready for a quick nap before departure.

She had initially planned to unbox everything that day and head off to her hometown the next morning. But she was so eager to see her grandparents again that the situation got unbalanced the minute she thought about it. All her belongings, and especially her winter clothes, could remain as they were until she came back to Dundee after the summer holidays.

She was not a fan of driving. She had never been, nor she will ever be, but as independent as she was, she needed to do things by herself that she would rather not do if she were with someone else. For such reason, she always planned her trips with time, always making sure that no matter how delayed they might become, she would not have to drive long distances at night-time. Such was her fear of driving in the dark in fact that, despite the one-hour nap she had taken, she got to Pitlochry long before the sun had even started setting.

The fifty-two miles that separated her two homes were gone faster than she had expected. It was true she loathed driving, but to make her road trips more pleasant, she always sang the whole time. She would never sing in public, but when she was all by herself, it was something completely different. She was aware of how bad of a singer she was, but when it was only her ears that had to listen to it, she just did not care.

As a scientist, she found the process of creation from scratch quite complicated. She had never had a good hand for anything artistic, from painting to playing any instrument, so she had always admired every single person that had been gifted those skills. However, something she was quite good at was at remembering quotes and the lyrics to any song. Anything that regarded words actually. Although as shy as she was, she had not let many people know about that side of hers, and thus words had remained her little secret.

'*The number of things we can express through words equals infinity. Mastering the process of putting them in the right order is a gift on its own as well.*' She had repeated to herself as she had gotten into her car, ready to kick start her summer holidays.

The town looked busy because of all the holidaymakers that had decided to spend their holidays inland. That busy indeed, that she had a little bit of trouble to find a spot to park her second-hand car. She was starting to get quite anxious about not finding a place when luck shined on her .The third time she drove past the main road of the neighbourhood, she found a parking place. She skilfully parked her car two houses away from her grandparents', took her belongings from the boot and headed herself to the house.

'Hello!?' greeted Eileen when she opened the front door. 'I'm back…!' she added while leaving her cases by the cupboard under the stairs. She then took her shoes off and put on her old comfortable Scottish rugby-themed slippers. When she turned around she realised that her grandmother had walked into the hall to welcome her home: 'Evening grandma! How do you do? I am so happy to be back again. I have missed you a lot'. It was the longest she had been away from her grandparents, so all the emotions overflooded her the moment she saw her Leagsaidh again. Such was the case in fact, that she could not hold her tears when her grandmother said:

'Oh, sweethea't! It's so good to see ye. Come hug this old lady, ye will'.

Feeling homely welcomed by her grandmother's strong accent, Eileen walked the few inches that laid between them, and hugged and kissed her grandmother for all the times they had not been able to do so for the last seven months. Happy tears kept running along their faces the whole time, which from the outside did not make it seem as though they were feeling as happy as they were. Or so thought her grandfather when he walked into the hall.

'Who would say ye were happy!' exclaimed Alick when he saw the scene from the dining room doorframe. Neither Eileen nor her grandmother had noticed him until he spoke. The moment they did however, they undid their hug so Eileen could offer one arm for him to join them. Without any hesitation, he shortened the distance that separated them and joined the hug.

Not even today can they tell how long they hugged for, but they do vividly remember the connection they felt for as long as it lasted. Eileen was the only grandchild of the Bruce marriage, so joy overfilled them whenever she returned home. The opposite held true for when she left the house, but they all tried their best not to think about that beforehand.

After recomposing, they all got ready for dinner. They were to have it at a much later hour than they all usually did, but that did not stop them from chitchatting for hours. They talked about everything and nothing, catching up on each other's lives and forgetting about the fact that time was a free soul that ran at its own pace, which resulted in them going to bed past midnight.

'Look at the hour!' exclaimed Eileen when she glanced at the clock hanging on the wall. 'I can't believe I'm not feeling sleepy at a…' she said, although a yawn took over her right then, which made her lose all credibility. 'I'll help you get ever…'.

'No, ye go to bed righ' now,' interrupted Alick. 'I'll get this sorted out meself'.

'It'll take us haaaaaalf…the time if I help you,' replied Eileen, yawning again.

'Ye can't even talk, Eileen. Ye are tired. Please, go to bed straight away' said Leagsaidh, caressing her grandchild on her arm.

Assuming that arguing with her grandparents would not make any difference, Eileen decided to kiss them goodnight and head upstairs to her old room. Halfway up the stairs, she realised she had left her suitcase in the hall, but because she still had some old clothes in her room, she decided it was not worth the risk going downstairs again. As the winter clothes she had left at her new apartment in Dundee, everything she had brought to Pitlochry could wait for the next day.

Once upstairs, she went to the bathroom to brush her teeth and comb her hair. Out of the three bathrooms in the house, the one on the second storey was her favourite one. It had a skylight that allowed for a beautiful view of the Scottish night. And even when it rained it looked stunning. It allowed for natural light to come inside the house, which made everything acquire a unique look.

Once done, she went to her room. She had played strong in front of her grandparents, but the truth was that she was feeling really tired. So much, that she was unaware of how full her bedroom looked until she switched on the lights. Afraid of having been tricked by her subconscious however, she blinked her eyes repeatedly. But nothing changed. Her room was indeed full of balloons.

There were balloons of different sizes and colours, but none seemed to have a note to highlight the fact as to why they were there. And just as she was about to run downstairs to ask her grandparents, she saw that there was an envelope lying on her old desktop. She walked towards it and then stretched her arm to get hold of it. She recognised the flickering handwriting of her grandfather straight away.

'You know me like no other, grandpa,' said Eileen when she flipped the envelope around. Her grandfather had drawn some small letters and books all over it.

She then laid on her bed to read the letter that she had just retrieved from the inside of the envelope.

1

The day after she arrived in Pitlochry, she woke up at almost lunchtime. She had been sent to bed past midnight, but she had not fallen asleep until around 2 a.m. After having read the letter that her grandfather had left for her, she had spent almost two hours thinking of what she had always thought about doing, but that she had never found neither the determination nor the inspiration for. As a result, she had woken up feeling really sleepy that morning.

She was so happy by the coast enjoying herself, but there was nothing like going back to one's roots for a full battery recharge. It had not been invented yet, something as glorious as a grandmother's meal. Eileen was a cook herself, as long as her always busy schedule allowed her to spend some time in the kitchen, but her grandmother's meals were the best. She did not recall a single time that she had not enjoyed something prepared by Leagsaidh, whereas her owns… more than once she had had to eat things that if anybody else had cooked them, she would have not dared to try.

'The perks of living by myself' she thought while getting out of bed and opening her room window for the air to get renewed. She let the fresh air welcome her to a brand new day for a couple of seconds, and then decided that the only thing that would truly wake her up would be a morning shower. She turned around to head to her wardrobe to pick up some clothes, and as she was about to open one of the cupboards, she glanced at her grandfather's letter lying on the floor, right next to her bed. Assuming that it had slipped from her hands as she had fallen asleep, she kneeled and grabbed it:

Dear Eileen,

Welcome back!

Grandma and I have thought about setting up your room for your arrival as a surprise for our young working adult. You will never get to experience this first time ever again, so enjoy it to the fullest. You coming back is a reason good enough for us to party. At the end of the day, you are our only grandchild, and we can't be happier to have you with us again. We hope you enjoy your time inland.

Lots of love,

Your grandparents.

PS: I know you are a very young talented woman, and that anyone in their right mind would love to have you around. But I also know you are a very reserved individual. I believe you should let the world see what is inside of you. Let everyone experience that your heart has beaten for, for as long as you can remember. Bring that dreamer back, do it for this old man.

She had never been a very emotional individual, but we all go through that phase at some point in our lives. She had grabbed the letter with galloping tears finding their way to her eyes so naturally, by the time she finished rereading it, they had already found their way out. She had never been good at showing her emotions in public, but she was a completely different person when in her room. Whenever she felt she had no eyes on her, she felt she could truly be her. The silent freedom her room provided her with, allowed for her brain to lose control in favour of her heart. That was when she would cry or dance or sing as her body asked her to.

Still whimpering, she folded the letter back into the envelope. She then took some clean garments and headed to the bathroom. Her stomach was complaining because it had not been filled for a long time, but she still had to get that much-needed shower.

The skylight in the bathroom welcomed her by letting the sunlight get through it, which made her smile widely. A day that started like that could not let anyone down. She then took a quick shower, put on some joggers and a T-shirt and went downstairs to join her grandparents.

'Ye were tired, ye! C'me jein us h're, sweethhea't' said her Leagsaidh while standing up to serve her grandchild a full dish of traditional Scottish haggis. 'Ye eat that all or ye don' move' she warned Eileen, mimicking the tone she used to use when Eileen was a kid. Unfortunately for her grandparents, she had never had a good appetite.

'That I will grandma. Thanks,' said Eileen while sitting down at her spot. She had sat at that very same end of the table for as long as she could remember. 'By the way, thank you so much for my welcome back balloons. I was not expecting any of that whatsoever. You did make my day last night' she added before taking a big mouthful.

Her grandparents looked at each other and smiled before Alick replied: 'It is ye who make ou' days eve'y day, sweethea't. And have ye given a thought to *it*?' he quickly added, knowing full well that Eileen would understand what he was talking about.

'I have indeed. And of course I am into it! I have been thinking about it for months now, years probably. But I have been in this busy spiral lately that has forced me away from what somehow makes me, me,' she said, suddenly becoming a bit sad, for she had not realised how much she had missed doing that until she had voiced it. 'Actually, I have had this idea for weeks now. I just wished I were able to make it real' she added, more to herself than to her grandfather.

'What is it? I bel'eve ye've got 3 weeks off fer ye to work on it' said Alick, winking his eye at Eileen.

'I don't know grandpa… I mean, I believe that if I were able to make it real, it'd be an awesome book. I haven't read anything like what I have in mind ever before. But I still struggle trying to make up the story. Besides, I have never been able to go that far in my writing,' she added downheartedly.

'Don't ye think like that girl!' replied Alick. He then took a few seconds to reconsider his arguments before he added: 'How 'bout ye tell me what ye've got in mind? I'd be more than happy to help ye out.' Afterwards, and in order to persuade her, he moved closer to her, and kindly caressed his grandchild on her arm. He was aware she was not one to be touched that freely, yet he knew she made exceptions for those she truly cared about.

Letting her grandfather do, Eileen pondered the options she had, and whether or not telling her grandfather about the ideas she had had would be the best of them all. She could try and explain what she had envisioned, although that would probably spoil the whole concept. She also thought about explaining how she had gotten the idea, wishing that he would get the point straight away, but she declined that idea the minute she had it. All in all, she had been left with just one option: producing the manuscript and letting him give her his feedback. Besides, that way, he would become a key element in the writing process, as his comments would help shape the story.

She gave it a long thought, but she could not reach any other conclusion and thus told her grandfather that he would officially become her assistant. Alike Eileen had expected, he agreed the minute she proposed the offer, which made her laugh and say: 'You needn't agree with me on everything I say, grandpa'.

'I'm not agreeing on doing it because ye suggested it, young lady,' said Alick, defensively. 'It's jus' that I think it's a great idea. Besides, I guess that would be the closest I'll ever be to writing a story meself' he quickly added, understanding that he had not sounded convincing at all.

'Is that it? Really? Give me a wink if you're lying!' challenged Eileen, suspicious. As an only grandchild, she knew that she just needed to blink her eyes a few times for her to get away with her whims. Assuming that him not blinking meant he was being honest, Eileen decided to trust his word. 'As you've said, I've got three weeks off for me to focus on the project. I believe it's better if we arranged timetables though. I shall have one for me to write, and you shall have another one to revise my writing. If we both commit to them, we shall be done by the time I must head to the coast again'.

'Sounds fai' to me,' said Alick.

As a reply to his commitment, Eileen jumped off her chair and headed to her room to pick up her laptop. She knew she was being too optimistic thinking that she would be able to produce a whole novel in just three weeks when she had not written anything for years. And even more when those she had written in the past had not been long enough as to be considered more than tales. However, she had the feeling that that summer would be different. She should at least give it a try. She had had an idea for months, and no plans were awaiting for her at Pitlochry, so what could go wrong?

Eileen and her grandfather agreed that the writing would be done in the mornings, whereas the revision and discussion would be twice or thrice a week in the evenings, depending on how many pages Eileen had been able to produce. That very first day however, as she had gotten up so late, they had agreed to go for a walk around the neighbourhood, as that might help her get some extra ideas.

'Ye reckon the village doesn' show like this when eve'ybody is wo'king, righ'?' said Alick matter-of-factly a few minutes into their walk. 'I me'n, when holidaymakers are at their places. We don' attract employers. The area is condemned,' he added mournfully.

Eileen knew her grandfather was right. She herself, who had been born and raised in the area, had had to leave to find a living. She had first moved to Edinburgh at the age of 17 (she had been born in late November) to study at university. After graduating, she had found herself a job in Dundee that she was enjoying a lot. Nevertheless, and even though she liked it at her new location because of all the opportunities it offered, she was sad she could not make a living in her hometown.

'When ye become a famous writer, ye could c'me back. No worries 'bout that,' said Alick as though he had just read through his grandchild's skull.

'You've got very high expectations about me, grandpa,' said Eileen, blushing. When she first started writing at the age of nine, she dreamed of producing such good stories as her favourite author, JK Rowling, so she could be able to become as famous as her. She knew however that the difference between her and JK was that people had not had anyone to compare JK with, so the sky had been the limit.

'I don' see but what it is,' said Alick, gleefully. 'Anyway, I know we had agreed fer me to jus' read the manuscript as ye produce it, but... couldn' this old man get a glimpse of what is to come? I'm certainly curious 'bout how ye gonna work'.

'I guess there is nothing wrong with me telling you how I plan to work. After all, whenever we find a book at the book shop, we get to read a few lines about the story to create expectations,' said Eileen. 'So... what I plan to do is, I will first go through a story I wrote when I was doing my A-levels, so I can get a contest for the characters. I will then use those same characters for a completely different story. Thus yes, I first need to reread it and take notes about the main aspects of each character. I would then be ready to start creating the new story' she added.

'Could I have a read?' I'm intrigued 'bout what the characters looked like when ye created them,' suggested Alick. He enjoyed her writing so much he could not keep to his word of not trying to take things from her beforehand.

Eileen had not foreseen her grandfather would be asking for that, so she had to give it a thorough thought. She did not want to spoil the new story, but him reading the somehow origin of it would not necessarily do that. Besides, what if he were right and that could be helpful? What if him reading the story could give her new ideas for the now growing one? 'I guess you could, yes. I shall give it a read first to correct minor mistakes though'.

'Fair enough. Do ye reckon ye could be done by nigh' time?' asked Alick, nervous for his dare.

'I guess I could, yes,' replied Eileen among laughs. 'We shall head home now though, or you'll have to wait 'til tomorrow morning'.

- I -

Red-haired Nora enjoyed her summer holidays as much as other fifteen-year-olds did. She was a good student and got extremely good grades at school, but this did not stop her from wanting summer to come as fast as possible.

She wanted to be a normal girl, and she was in most ways indeed. But there was something that made her different: she was a wonder girl playing the piano. She had played the piano for as long as she could remember. She liked it, but it was also tiring at times…

She came from a humble family from northern Scotland and had moved to London to take piano lessons with one of the best teachers of the moment. When she had heard Mr Ross wanted to be her teacher, she had been completely unable to hide her excitement. She had started packing all her belongings the minute her parents had told her the good news, but the reality she found down south was not the fairy tale she thought it would be. After a couple of months, she was not that enthusiastic. Her timetable had been filled with must-do activities that she enjoyed on their own, but that became sort of wearisome when there was no other way to get through the day but by doing them.

She often wondered what would have happened if she had not been an only child, or whether she had not stood out due to her piano skills, but it was already too late for her to find out what her life would have turned into. Luckily for her however, she did feel the freedom of no timetables when she was allowed at her grandmother's in Scotland. She was aware that her parents did not approve of her not going through her must-do activities, but her grandmother was on her side, and that meant the argument was always balanced in favour of her interests. Like that one time a few years before when she had started feeling hungry and had gone downstairs to grab something to eat, to find herself eavesdropping from the corridor. Her grandmother and her parents were having a very heated conversation in the kitchen. She had realised they were talking about her before she heard her name, yet she had to quit listening the moment she noticed someone was sobbing. With drowned eyes, she had run upstairs to her room, where she had locked the door, wishing for the argument downstairs to finish the sooner, the better.

A couple of hours after that, her grandmother Mary had found her lying in her bed. They had always been very close, so they had not needed more than a look into each other's eyes to find out what they were dealing with. Their bond was so special, that even though Nora never voiced all the questions her then out-of-control brain was coming up with, she got all of them answered. When Mary finished her explanations however, they were both in tears, and thus were completely unable to talk. Their sobs and running noses prevented them from speaking, but not from bear-hugging each other. Because there are times when no words are needed to express one's feelings.

That bear-hug they shared that day lasted long enough to strengthen the bond they had shared for as long as Nora could remember. Hence, from that day on, that bond did not stop from growing bigger and stronger, as they worked on it by pouring their feelings onto the dedicated letters that they sent to each other. Just like the one that Nora had received that very same morning:

Dear Nora,

I am pleased to hear you are doing well at school. Keep on like that, sweety!

There is not much time left until you come around, so I have already started preparing your room. I am afraid it will not look like the one you have got in London, but I am trying my best to make it cosy for you, so you don't notice.

I haven't got room for your piano-keyboard at my place –I know you wanted me to convince your parents to stop playing it during your stay here, but they have not gone through. Sweety, I am afraid you will have to practice for a couple of hours a day. Since I don't have one of my own, your parents have agreed for you to go to my friend Amy's to practice on her grandchild's. He is your age, so you might become good friends with him.

Please, tell your parents to let me know when exactly you are coming; I have got yet another surprise for you that still needs prepping.

Lots of love,

Granny Mary.

Due to the delay in the post-mail, that letter had arrived just a few days before their planned departure at the end of the week. Nora had read it over ten times, trying to find out whether her grandmother had left any secret hints to what the surprise might be. But because by the tenth attempt she still had nothing, she had decided to let the investigation go. Although reticent, she had accepted the waste of time that pursuing the analysis any further would be. Assuming her grandmother would let her know the minute she laid her feet in Scotland, she had deemed it convenient filing the letter in the box she had handcrafted for the purpose. Then, she had headed downstairs to join her parents for lunch. She was aware that they were not approving the situation, yet she was determined to not let anything get in between her and whatever her grandmother had planned for that summer break. Thus, before leaving the corridor behind, she swallowed saliva and opened the door as calmly as her raising heartbeat allowed her to. She then asked her parents whether they had done as her grandmother had requested. She had been very careful to not leak anything that might make them suspicious about the surprise. She had a feeling that they were better left aside on that topic.

'Oh… sorry, Nora. I haven't had time for that at all. We've been running from meeting to meeting for the last two days. But I promise I'll phone her after lunch,' said her mother, pinky-promising her. 'Also…, once you are done having your meal, could you please go upstairs and finish up your French homework? I've gotten an email from the academy requesting it to wrap up the course'.

'Will do, mum,' said Nora. She was so used to being asked to do things, that she had since long learned to not let the circumstances determine her mood. After all, in just a few days she would be back in Scotland!

It took them more than half a day to get to granny Mary's by car. But for Nora, it was all worth it. For the next two weeks, she would be allowed to do whatever she wanted, whenever she wanted to. She could stay up until late, sleep in, skip both breakfast and brunch, or simply enjoy the scenery. She had been obsessed with the Scottish landscape for as long as she could remember. The northern part of the island looked completely different from the southern half. Up there, even the air felt different.

The closer they got to the small village however, the faster both the excitement to be around her grandmother again, and the fatigue built up. Her legs were feeling numb, and her stomach was craving dinner. She was used to travelling long distances, but that did not mean she did not loathe the last minutes of every journey. At the end of the day, that was when one was too tired to even protest, but also too excited to eventually reach their destination.

'That new billboard is as big as the village itself!' exclaimed Nora's father, breaking up her daydreaming bubble.

Nora had been dealing with her excitement versus fatigue dilemma, and thus had not realised that from where they were, they could already see the first houses. She looked outside the window and damned her short-sightedness. They would have to get much closer before she would be able to read anything.

Yet when she could read it, she thought her eyes were tricking her. She was feeling so tired that should have she been in a desert, she would have seen oasis everywhere. Claiming for her rational self to prevail over her tiredness, she rubbed her eyes and waited for an image to be formed again. But the new image did not differ on anything from the first one she had gotten. She had no other option but to agree that there was no trick whatsoever. What she was seeing was exactly what she was supposed to be seeing.

The huge billboard her father had pointed out, which was right next to the one that read the name of the village, was plain white except for just three words: *Welcome back, Nora!* She had known that her grandmother had planned a surprise for her, but she never thought it would include the whole village! Although she had to agree that one never really knew what to expect from her grandmother. However crazy the idea, if Mary wanted to carry it out, then she would find the way to do it.

Once they drove past the huge billboard, Nora let the excitement take over her. Laying back, she closed her eyes and recreated in her mind the way to her grandmother's... *'first to the left, three houses and again to the left, five more houses and then to the right...'*. She had felt her heartbeat raise with every turn, but she forced her eyes closed until she felt her father stopped the engine. She was finally back! When she opened her eyes she saw her grandmother was waiting at the bench by the entrance, so she hurried to unfasten her seatbelt, jump off the car and run towards her grandmother. Despite the warmth that every single letter from Mary had filled her heart with, there was nothing like an actual bear-hug. Because it is never about how much we tell someone we love them, but how much we make them feel loved.

'Honey, we are off to Berlin tomorrow,' said dad, leaving Nora's suitcase by the entrance door. 'I needn't add you behave properly, do I?' he added, planting a soft kiss on Nora's forehead.

'I thought you were at least staying tonight!' exclaimed Mary, searching for her keys in the pocket of her skirt.

'No mum, we are not. We have got business meetings in Germany, so we have booked ourselves a hotel room in Glasgow for as to fly to Berlin tomorrow morning' said Nora's mum, closing the door behind her. 'We'll join you for dinner today, but we are leaving right afterwards. Although… could we talk to your friend Abby first? We'd like to thank her in person for lending Nora her piano. Besides, I'd like to check with her whether the timetable I've arranged suits her…'.

'We have gone over this a hundred times so far,' said Mary, clearly making an effort to sound as firm as she could. 'She is both on holiday and at my place. She will do whatever I say. And I do not want to argue,' she added when her son-in-law tried to speak.

Nora witnessed the tense encounter keeping her breath. She was aware of the many sacrifices her parents had had to face so she would have everything she did. And she was very pleased for it all, do not think she was not. But she was also sorry they could not see they were taking her teenage years away from her. She was responsible on her own, and thus, she knew that the best thing she could do was to take a break from time to time.

Despite that uncomfortable moment, the soiree felt nice. They enjoyed their dinners, which made Nora and her parents recover from the long journey. But as much as they wanted to stretch it out, Nora's parents needed to head to Glasgow in order to keep on with their duties.

'Dinner was delicious, mum,' said Nora's mum, taking her purse from the hook, already next to the entrance door. 'I wish we could enjoy your meals a little bit longer, but work is work. See you both in a couple of weeks!' she added, sounding sorry to have to leave only a few hours after they had arrived.

Mary and Nora greeted them goodbye from the front yard, and once they saw the car disappearing at the nearest crossroad, they shut the gate close and went back to the living room.

For the first time in six months, Nora had nothing planned ahead of her, if we intentionally exclude her few piano practices, of course. Her must-do activities would be non-existing for over two weeks! She wished she could stay at her grandmother's in her current situation for longer, but she had to remain sensible about her situation. After all, she had been left with only two options: she could either complain about it or make the most out of it. It was just up to her whether she wanted to enjoy her summer or regret she did not embrace the situation.

'May I get my suitcase unpac…?' tried to ask Nora.

'And how about we go for a walk? Let's leave the *being-formal-behaviour* for when you head down south again. Being naughty sometimes is soul healing, you know,' interrupted Mary, caressing Nora's face.

Nora had only been at her grandmother's during her holidays periods, as before moving to London, she had already been living in Glasgow because of her parents' job duties. However, and even though she had visited the village every single year of her life, she did not have any close friends there. Since she had moved to London, she had not been able to spend much time at her grandmother's. Instead, she had had to spend most of her school holidays travelling to different countries to perform the plays that Mr Ross so carefully chose for her. Therefore, she was all ready to embrace new friendships.

Five minutes after they had left the house, Nora found the courage to ask her grandmother about the surprise she had mentioned in her last letter. By the way Mary had reacted to her parents talking about the huge billboard that had welcomed them to the small village, she had realised that it was not the big surprise that had been awaiting her. Or better, not the whole of it.

'Oh, that! I thought you'd never ask!' exclaimed Mary, laughing. 'I got you this…' she added, handing Nora a rectangular birthday-wrapped parcel. Since they had left the house, Nora had been curious as to why her grandmother had brought such a big bag with her, but she had not pointed it out. Once Nora opened the parcel, Mary continued talking: 'It is a book that gathers a bunch of Scottish legends. It is not a new book, I know, but don't moan just yet. I reckon I was running out of ideas for a surprise, so I thought you might like doing some exploring. My dad granted it to me when I was your age, and I think it is time for you to have it. I think I don't spoil anything if I say one of the legends is located in this village actually'.

2

K *nock, knock…*

'Come in,' said Eileen. Even though the night before she had gone to bed late, she had gotten up early that morning. She had worked in correcting the minor mistakes her former red-haired Nora story had so she could email it to her grandfather. She had kept her word, so she was free to start focusing on her new project. She liked the idea she had come up with from the very beginning, but she was uncertain as to what extent she would be able to accomplish her goal. She had a lot of fresh new ideas for it, which made her really excited about trying out the author life. But she was as concerned about whether she would be able to put her thoughts into words.

'I know we've agreed fer the discussions to be in the evenings, bu' I need talking 'bout it now,' said Alick from the doorframe. When his grandchild nodded her head yes, he entered the room, leaving the door open.

'How deep into the story are you, grandpa?' asked Eileen in laughs. She had written that story a while ago, and even though she was really proud of it, she did not think there were much to talk about.

'Nora had jus' been handed the book' replied Alick. Seeing Eileen was about to complain, he silenced her with a flip of his hand and resumed: 'I know I am bu' a' the ve'y beginning, bu' I jus' wanted to say tha' I have really liked it so far. I've go' high expectations on what is to c'me'.

Eileen appreciated the kind words of her grandfather, although she was again suspicious about his good intentions She pondered the possibility of challenging him again to wink an eye if he were lying, but by the brightness his eyes shined with, she realised he was speaking from the bottom of his heart.

'I know you really want to help me, grandpa, but I must really get to work right now. I need to type on that laptop,' she said, pointing backwards at her desktop 'as much as I can, so I can give you new material every day. I am just starting to realise how much work it is to be an author', she whispered, more to herself than to her grandfather.

'Shall we discuss it today, shall we no'?' asked Alick, a bit saddened. He was really excited about being able to participate in the writing of what he hoped would be the next Scottish best-seller.

Eileen stood up from the desk chair and confirmed that they would indeed discuss the novel later that day. At the same time, she slowly pushed him out of her room. She then turned around and faced her desk. She had a lot of work to do.

- II -

Even though the village where granny Mary lived was not very big, for Nora, the perception of time and space had been drawn out since she had received her copy of *All Scottish Legends*. All she could think about was getting home to start wolfing it down.

And that was exactly what she did when they got back home. The moment they stepped into the hall, she took her shoes off and ran upstairs to her room. There was not anyone else in the house other than her grandmother, yet she felt the urge to be on her own.

Once upstairs, she locked herself in her bedroom and kneeled. It was the first time she had ever had such an old book in her hands, so she was curious about what its general look would be like, and whether she would be able to work out how old it really was. Thus, she tried to flip the pages to see whether or not it had pictures, but to her surprise, the book would not open. She found that quite strange, although it was nothing compared to what happened right afterwards. The moment she stopped forcing the book to open, it jumped off her hands by a force that seemed to have come from within. It hit the floor, and bounced like a ball several times, before laying open at the very beginning. The sudden movement had startled her really badly, but unfortunately for her, that had not been it. The minute the book remained still, the blank pages started to be filled by a handless ink. She looked at the book, completely unable to see what the new content was, but not daring to come any closer at the same time. However, because after a few minutes nothing odd happened again, she came closer to the book to discover there was now a handwritten letter on display:

Dear dauntless reader,

If you got hold of this book, it might be because someone considered you a worthy owner of it. We congratulate you on that, although we shall point out, that anyone who opens this book shall be ready to explore, for there is nothing worse than restraining curiosity towards the unknown. As an attention-catcher, we'd say that the Legends gathered in this book are as true as the origin of life, whichever version you decide to believe.

As payment for us offering this letter for free, we strongly urge you, that should you be miles away from where the Legends took place, please try not to read them. Due to the extraordinary events that originated in some of them, every time they are reread, the story might start all over again for the protagonists. And you may not be surprised if we guarantee there is extreme suffering in some of them.

Therefore, we cannot promise that by you submitting yourself to the Legends, you would not suffer any consequences. Although we warn you, that you must take into consideration that once you do submit, there is no way back. There will be no dubious or evasive behaviours allowed. Once you do submit, you will be in, forever. Hence, it is up to you whether or not you are willing to take the risk.

Yet, do not think of us as demons. We do not want to scare you off. We are aware that all we have said so far is not very encouraging. But that is just because we left the best for last. By reading the legend of choice, you would not only experience what we have explained above. You will also be provided with information, so do not be desperate. Bear in mind however, that knowing too much is sometimes as dangerous as knowing too little. Despite all that, we encourage you to bear with us.

Yours sincerely,

The protagonists.

After having read the warning, because there was not any other way to describe that, or at least Nora could not find it, she started shaking. How dare her grandmother gift her such a potentially dangerous book? She was not a fairy-tale type of girl, and she was not really into magic either; not at her age, for Goodness sake! But the book jumping off her hands had been as tangible as the fact she was red-haired.

When she recomposed, she thought of going downstairs to have a serious chat with her grandmother. The book was not new, that Nora knew. Her grandmother had said, that her father had gifted it to her, so there was a slight possibility that Mary herself had been involved with it, somehow. Was she one of the authors, or had the book been written long before she had been born? Had she lied about her dad gifting it to her? Had she succeeded in unravelling the hidden mysteries? There were so many questions galloping to her brains, that she was not sure whether she would be able to remember them all by the time she would reach her grandmother.

'*I might as well just write them down*' thought Nora. Realising that that was the best option she had, she walked towards the backpack that she had left by the wardrobe. She had packed a pencil case and a couple of music notebooks, just in case she came up with a new melody while at her grandmother's. In the absence of any other notebook right then, she pulled out a couple of the staved pages and started writing as fast as she could.

And then, all of a sudden, when she was not even halfway through writing down all the questions she had, she heard a sound that seemed to come from the book itself. If Nora had not witnessed some of the strange capabilities of that book, she would have not paid attention to it whatsoever. But the situation was odd enough as to get startled by the most trivial things.

Folding the scribbled staved page and putting it into one of the pockets of her jeans, together with the pen, she turned around very slowly to face the book again. The sound had not lasted very long, and it had stopped as suddenly as it had started, yet she was so sure it had been a harp melody she knew well, although she could not recall its title right then.

She stared at the book, ready to recognise any other melody that might come out of it. But nothing else happened. The book had laid open on the same page as it had been since it had opened itself, as though it was a normal one. She kept staring at it until she noticed something she had not seen before. Being as careful as she could, she took a step closer to the book, to find herself shakily staring at what she knew she would have nightmares with.

As she had so well guessed, the page did not exactly show as before. There were now some musical notes right beneath the signature. For someone who did not understand anything about music, they would have probably been meaningless, but Nora had a feeling that they would be vital for the upcoming events. She was so sure they had not just appeared on the page for no reason.

'You will also be provided with information, so do not be desperate' she silently mouthed, before finding the courage to eventually come into contact with the book. She flipped the cover shut, grabbed it with just two fingers, thus minimizing her contact with it, and barged her way out of her room.

3

Eileen had spent all morning locked in her room. Unfortunately however, she had not been able to write much, and even though she did not want it to, that was starting to weigh her down. She had a very clear idea in her head of what she wanted to do, yet she was completely unable to write it down as she wished she would. She had the feeling she was advancing much slower than she should, given her circumstances, so she decided to go downstairs to have something to eat.

But when she entered the kitchen, where her grandparents were setting up the table for lunch, she realised that she was not hungry. Or at least not food-wise. She had unconsciously driven herself to her grandfather for a much-needed chat.

'Only well nourishe' authors produce grea' novels. Let' have lunch now. We'll go fer a walk after tha',' said Alick without turning around, as though he had, again, read his grandchild's thoughts. That seemed to be a superpower of his.

'Grandpa, the truth is I am struggling with the writing. I know what I want to tell, but I find it difficult to do it in such a way that it is as exciting as it is in my head, if you know what I mean,' said Eileen, locking the fence after her.

'Don' ye whip yerself. No-one eve' said tha' being an author was easy,' said Alick. 'Ye're old enough to know tha' anything worth having is worth fighting fer, as well as tha' no beginning is easy. It's normal fer ye to have doubts now. And don' take me wrong, bu' ye'll have loads throughou' the whole process! Ye'll have yer ups and downs. Ye' ye'll succeed, as ye always have,' he added looking right into Eileen's eyes.

'I know, I know. I want to be as positive as sensible about the situation, but you must reckon you are biased because you love me, grandpa' replied Eileen. And, seeing her grandfather's reaction, she hurried to add: 'The thing is I have always written by myself, and most of what I have written has never been read. And I'm not surrounded by men of letters; I am self-taught. Maybe I am aiming for too much'.

'And who said aiming fer too much were bad? This old man migh' haven' been to university nor countries overseas, but he does recognise talen' when he sees it. I'm no' saying ye're good because ye're family to me, I'm saying tha' because it's true! And the sooner ye realise tha', the sooner ye'll succeed. Besides, what is it to be taught 'bout writing?' he asked. He wanted Eileen to realise that she had been gifted the ability to write, and he wanted her to realise it by herself. Thus, to promote that brainstorming in his grandchild, he added: 'It's by t'ying and failing that ye'd find yer path. Also, ye shouldn't aim to be the next bestseller author, or at least not fer the meantime. Let ye surprise yerself by yer abilities, but don' whip the hope out of ye. What's meant to be, will be. Trust me'.

'*What if grandpa is right? What if I'm being too pessimistic too soon?*' she thought. Nobody had ever forced her to write, yet she had sometimes found it as the perfect way to pour herself out.

She was not one to phone a friend to talk for hours about her problems, nor anyone who would show off about her achievements. She was just someone who lived the moment and got surprised and excited about the most trivial things.

As with her grandfather however, she had always found it very difficult to hide anything from him. She had realised from a very young age that she could be her true self when he was around. He had had this sort of superpower to see through her skull just by looking into her eyes for as long as Eileen could remember, so it had been long since she had quit trying to hide anything from him. Although it had not been something she had always appreciated. As a teenager, she had had the urge to keep some things private, so she had more than once wished that she had not been that easy to read. Whereas now, she was really pleased with the special connection they shared.

'I reckon yer struggle, don' ye think I don', Eileen,' said Alick after having allowed her to think about it on her own. 'But ye know what yer name means…'.

'Bright, shining light,' they said in unison.

And after that, they laughed as though they had not done so in years. And that was as uplifting as strange in the eyes of others. But they did not care. It was true they had started laughing for no apparent reason, yet they were the only persons they had to give account to.

'C'me… on, grand…pa!' exclaimed Eileen breathless due to the laughs. 'Are you gonna tell me now that it is because of my name that I can do things? You're talking to a scientist who wouldn't take that, you know that, right?'.

'Ye scientists are a bit narrowed-minded sometimes,' said Alick, ending his laugh as suddenly as he had started it. 'Ye take all the magic frem life. Ye need a prove fer everything. Ye…'.

'We were gifted different skills, that's all, grandpa.' Eileen cut him off. 'Yet you'd agree with me that my fellow colleagues have done things to improve your life. We don't just take magic from life, we sometimes make it happen too' she added, a bit hurt and as laugh-less as her grandfather. 'And don't take me wrong. I'm not saying however that we are better than anyone else. We just see life through different spectacles. We see things that other people don't'.

'There ye have it' added Alick, recovering his smile.

'What do you mean *there you have it*?' asked Eileen, taken aback.

'Think about what ye've jus' said,' was all she got as a reply.

III

On her way downstairs, Nora started considering which were the best ways she could address the topic with her grandmother. She had always been very grateful for everything granny Mary had done for her, especially when she had confronted her parents whenever she had deemed it necessary. But that had been too much. How dare she get her involved in something that could report her consequences, however dangerous they could be? The protagonists had stated that very clearly! Had she gone completely out of her mind?

'Oh… Hi, Nora!'. Realising that Nora had been taken aback by the fact there was someone else with her, Mary quickly added: 'this is Mark. Mark, this is my grandchild, Nora'.

'*Awesome,*' thought Nora. She felt the urge to discuss the topic with her grandmother, so much that she did not feel like dedicating her time to meeting someone new. She had been eager to make close friends, but the timing was just not right. She did not feel like she had herself put together as to do so. Regardless of that however, she dried her sweaty hands on her jeans, mumbled a shy *hi* to Mark, and then turned to face her grandmother: 'Granny…, I actually wanted to talk to you about..mm…something. Could we go to the kitchen, please?'.

'I'm afraid not,' said Mary. She had not said it rudely, but to Nora, it felt as though an ice bucket had been emptied over her shoulders. 'Haven't you always said how eager you were to make close friends up here? Then don't miss this opportunity! Go outside, and enjoy yourself' added Mary, glancing at the *All Scottish Legends* copy that Nora had in her hands.

It had not passed unnoticed to Nora that her grandmother had stared at the book, which made her even more eager to want to discuss the topic with her. However, she had to agree that if her grandmother had said *no*, then there was nothing to do about it. And that was so damning frustrating. She knew well that Mary was not someone to be contradicted. Thus, as much as she despised the idea, she forfeit in her attempts.

'I was gonna go out for a walk with my pals, and since your grandma had told mine that you were around already, I was wondering whether you'd like to join us' said Mark after a very awkward silence. Nora had not forgotten about his presence, yet she would have preferred that their first encounter had been in complete different circumstances. She was sorry she might scare him away due to her being in a bit of an unfriendly mood.

'Al...alright then. Wait here. I'll take this upstairs,' she said, lifting her right hand to show him her *All Scottish Legends* copy. 'I might as well put some shoes on' she added, pointing at her bare feet.

'If I were you, I'd bring it with me,' said Mary while turning around. After that, she simply left the living room, not giving a single chance to be asked any other question.

Nora looked alternately from the spot her grandmother had occupied, to Mark, who looked as puzzled as she did. She hoped for something to happen so that she would understand the situation. But nothing seemed to change.

'I'll go get my shoes and a backpack then. Just a sec,' said Nora.

'I reckon that was weird, but your grandma is a cool granny. Mine has been friends with her for years now,' said

Mark while holding the fence gate for Nora. Realising he had taken her aback, he asked in laughs: 'You've no idea who I am, do you?'.

'I'm sorry, but no, I don't', replied Nora, a bit ashamed of him having realised that just by her look. She could not control her facial expressions sometimes.

'I'm Amy's grandchild,' he said. 'The one who was supposed to lend you the piano…' he hurried to add.

'Oooh. Now I get you! Nice to meet you, and sorry for… well… that' she said, pointing backwards towards her grandmother's house. 'What do you mean though by *supposed to*?' she added. She had not quite understood why he had used the past tense.

'Our grannies have planned for us to do something… different. Yeah, let's use that word. Di-ffe-rent,' he said, mouthing the word *different* very slowly, syllable by syllable. 'But don't take me wrong. You're welcome to play four-hands with me at my grandma's any time you want. I doubt we'll have any time for that whatsoever, but the offer is there, you know. Besides, aren't you tired of playing? I've heard you've toured Europe performing in concerts. It's good to have a break from time to time, you know'.

Nora was about to reply, but she closed her mouth altogether when she realised Mark was probably right. She was a pianist because she enjoyed it, not because anyone had forced her into it. She was aware she had always had a natural talent for it in fact, but her lectures had lately become more and more demanding. And aged fifteen, the possibility of doing something out of the ordinary sounded much more appealing to her. That much in fact, that her unfriendly mood started lifting by the sole thought of it. Could anything go wrong at all?

'Mark, you've got a very strong accent. Are you Scottish?' she asked. Ice-breaker questions were one of her many strong points.

'I was born in Belfast, but my whole family comes from Inverness, so I guess I am, somehow,' he said. He had not seen that question coming, yet he liked Nora was starting to relax. 'Why do you ask though?'.

'Ice-breaker?' she replied, giggling. 'By the way, what do you know about that book my grandma asked me to bring with me?'.

'The *All Scottish Legends*, you mean?'.

'Indeed. I had just been gifted it. Have you read it?' asked Nora, wishing for him to have more information than she did. After all, she had not mentioned the title of the book, yet he had seemed to have recognised it quite fast.

'No, I haven't,' replied Mark. 'But I have also been gifted it not so long ago. And so have Theresa and Gabe. You know, the twins that live across the street from your granny's...?' he added, as though that was a hint for her to remember who they were. Seeing the uncertain look that Nora looked at him with however, he resumed: 'anyways. All our grandmas are friends, so I guess they wanted their offspring's offspring would hang out together'.

Mark's witticism made Nora laugh. He was not just easy to talk to, but he was also fun to be around. He seemed to always have a quirky comment for the tense moments, which was so uplifting, given the circumstances. And above all, she was happy she was fitting in. She had dreamed so many times about making close friends at her grandmother's, that she was afraid she would not enjoy it as much as she had wished she would.

They kept with the chitchat until they got to the park by the river. Apparently, Mark had agreed with the twins to meet there.

'Pals, may I introduce you to Nora, Mary's grandchild. A world-famous pianist,' said Mark, bowing in a very jester-like way. He exaggerated the reverence so much, that by the time he stood up again, Nora's face was as red as her hair. To her surprise however, that did not but make Mark roar with laughter.

'You, moron!' exclaimed Theresa. She gave Mark a very serious look while she left aside her *All Scottish Legends* copy. Then, she stood up from the bench she was sitting on and offered Nora a handshake. 'Theresa; nice to meet you at last.' Grabbing her brother from the arm for him to stand up as well, she added: 'And this is my twin brother, Gabriel'.

'You call me Gabriel again, and you can consider yourself a dead woman,' said Gabe to his sister while standing up. Then, he turned around and, just like his sister, he offered his hand to Nora: 'Gabe'.

'Nice to meet you, too' greeted Nora again, while shaking his hand. The way Gabe looked into Nora's eyes while they shook their hands, made Nora feel both intimidated and intrigued about why that intensity on his eyesight. Although he completely broke the magic when he decided to play Mark's game: 'So... how many countries have you visited so far?'.

'*If only he hadn't used that quirky tone...,*' thought Nora, looking away from him. While doing so, she realised Theresa was not approving either of how both Mark and Gabe were behaving, so she gave her a reassuring look before saying: 'I've been to most countries in Europe, as well as to the USA and China. I'm next touring Oceania. But let's stop talking about me; I get that too often. We'd rather invest our time onto this' she said, pulling her *All Scottish Legends* copy out of her backpack.

The serious tone that Nora had used made both Mark and Gabe quit their laughs. Or maybe it had been at the sight of the *All Scottish Legends* copy. Either way, that made her giggle inside. She could be a buffoon herself as well.

And then, all of a sudden, Nora felt the joy being drawn from her. She also felt the urge to sit down, cross her legs and open her copy of the legends book on the only page that would open: the one that contained the protagonists' warning letter. She did not lift her eyes at all, and thus she could not see whether Mark, Theresa and Gabe were doing as she had. Although something deep down told her that they had felt the same as she had. Besides, and even though they had just met, she somehow knew that their copies read the same warning as hers. About the strange events that had happened right before the letter had been magically handwritten however, she doubted they had been alike for them all. Something inside of her told her that they were to work as one from then on, and so she started relating her experience. She mentioned how she had wanted to flip the pages but the book would not let her do that, as well as the fact it had jumped off her hands to open itself at the very beginning. She also pointed out the strange sound that had come from it only a few minutes later, and the musical notes doodles that seemed to have decorated the signature at the bottom of the page.

The other three listened to her with interest, as though that by listening to her story, they might get theirs shed some light on. Once Nora finished however, they all looked from one to another, waiting for someone else other than themselves to step ahead and share their story. After a few awkward seconds, Theresa took Nora's relay. With a shaky voice, that she was able to control after a few minutes, she shared what she had experienced with the book. She told them how she had broken the present paper it had been rapped on to, on that very moment, feel the urge to run to her room to start reading it. She also mentioned how she had not realised until she had locked the door after her, that the book cover had some cuts on it. She had not found that worthy of attention then, but it was something that disturbed her now. Besides, the memory of how the book had jumped off her hands became more and more vivid as she recalled it. She had just been so close to sliding her finger over one of the cuts, but all of a sudden, the book had been… gone! After that, her copy had behaved just like Nora's, which had made her startle and scream. She mentioned as well how she had had the feeling no one had been able to listen to her screaming, and had thus tried to run outside to her brother. Unfortunately for her, the door would not open, so she had been left with no other option than to face the book and succumb to it.

'Given that I couldn't leave my room, I kneeled on the carpet to be able to read what was written on that page. I tried to be as far as possible from the book, but my short-sightedness played against me,' she said, pointing at her glasses. 'I swear I was panicking so badly at the moment, that I would have collapsed if I had heard any weird sounds, let alone a random melody,' she added. By retelling the story, she was realising some things that had passed completely unnoticed to her. Clearly, the fact that she had found out that she had not been the only one who had experienced awkward situations was helping her to clear her thoughts. Finding her breath back, she continued talking: 'I eventually read the warning letter and decided I was not going to get involved with it. I'd return it to my grandma and have a nice and peaceful summer, thank you very much. But as I was thinking about how to tell her, I saw how the page was again doodled by an invisible hand. And that's when I started crying. I knew I was locked up in my room and that I couldn't get any help, so that was when I let myself go. It took me a while to recompose, and when I did, I saw what the finished doodles looked like,' she said, pointing at some footprints that laid on the same spot as Nora's musical notes.

Nora and Mark bent towards Theresa to have a closer look at what she was pointing at. Both of them recognised that the scrawls seemed to have been made by the same hand as theirs, for they all had that same imperfection on the round edges.

'I got some trees doodled on my copy,' interrupted Gabe all of a sudden, breaking up the established silence. 'I mean, I sort of experienced the same as you did, so what's the point on retelling? At the end of the day, what matters is my scrawls are trees, isn't it?'.

'I've got the impression every detail counts, though,' said Mark while offering his copy for the rest to see the scrawls that had been scribbled in it. He then added: 'Any wild guesses of what that could represent? I've no idea what mine is.'.

They all alternately looked from Mark's copy to each other, as though that would help in unravelling the mystery. But the looks they got back were as clueless as their own. And that was frightening, for they knew which was the only option they had left, should they truly want to find out what the scrawl represented.

4

The walk Eileen had gone on with her grandfather after lunch had left her with more questions than answers. She knew well that by answering the new questions, she would get exactly what she needed. But her problem was that she was clueless as to where to start from.

'*Think about what you've just said,*' had been the last words Alick had used. He had forced her into a small argument out of nowhere, which had taken Eileen completely by surprise. It had ended as suddenly as it had started, and Eileen doubted her grandfather was having rancour feelings about their confrontation. And above all, she hoped that deep down, her grandfather had made that hurtful comment for a reason.

'*If only he knew he needn't that type of comments to make me realise things… He could be more straightforward and not make a riddle out of everything,*' thought Eileen on her way upstairs. Their walk had lasted for about an hour and a half, and despite that little argument, it had been a soul-healing one. They had run into relatives and friends who they had not seen in months, for they, as Eileen, had had to move down south to find a living.

Once back in her room, she locked the door, put on her pyjamas and switched on her laptop. She was physically tired, but she had had an idea about her story that she could not let go of.

'Mo'ning, young lady! Do ye wan' a cup of coffee?' asked Alick when Eileen entered the kitchen for a late breakfast the next morning. She had worked on her computer non-stop since she had gotten home the day before, right until her grandfather had knocked on her room door to bring her dinner and wish her good night. She had completely lost track of time and thus had ended up going to bed really late. Completely unable to stop yawning, she sat at her spot and drank a big sip of her coffee.

'I didn't expect you'd be up by this time. You also went to bed really late last night,' said Eileen, grabbing a few homemade cookies from the platter. She was not a coffee person whatsoever, and thus needed something to balance the flavour. Regardless, she felt she needed something that would wake her up enough to get her through the day.

'I did indeed,' said Alick. 'Bu' I had the feeling we needed a talk before ye sta'ted wo'king,' he said, as though he had just mentioned it would rain in the evening.

'Grandpa, do you realise that I've got enough mental training with me trying to write a novel, as to deal with your riddles?' asked Eileen, swallowing one of the cookies.

'Don' ye be on the defensive, young lady. If I'm doing wha' I'm doing is to help ye,' said Alick. 'Anyway, what I wanted ye to know is that I like this version much more than the prevision one. One can tell there's a grown-up behind the scenes now. How come ye decided to change it?'.

Finishing up her coffee, Eileen breathed heavily and started laughing. She had been worried her grandfather was going to tell her off for something. Even though she was sure she had not done anything wrong.

'Well, our conversation during the walk left me pensive. I pondered what the options were, so I decided it might help me re-adapting something that I'd already finished, somehow. That way, besides trying out my capabilities as a mystery-keeping author, I could get to grow the characters' personalities a little bit more,' she said. She was only halfway through her re-adaptation of her old red-haired Nora story, yet she had emailed her grandfather the first chapters for him to start reading them.

'Ye see, this old man was righ' once again,' said Alick, caressing his grandchild's chin. One could tell how proud he was of her just by the brightness on his eyes. 'Ye'... well, we ain' following that schedule ye made' he added amongst laughs.

'Get stuffed!' exclaimed Eileen. 'We had agreed on working by schedules so that I could get hours with no interruptions. But... well, you know, they can be not followed should the aim require it'.

'Watch yer mouth, young lady,' said Alick. Indeed they had always had a close relationship, but he could not get used to the fact young people those days were using so many rude expressions. Accepting Eileen's apologetic face, he resumed: ''bout our topic... well, I've got the feeling now yer writing is definitely more mature. The essence of the forme' story is still there, one can tell, bu' I like how ye play with the breaks in the story-telling. How, in the end, ye make us relate to the characters. I haven' found it neither boring nor slow-moving, even if ye've considerably lengthened it. I'm curious about the next delivery ye make'.

Those words were for sure reassuring. Eileen had written that story when she was only seventeen and, just like her grandfather, she was liking best the new version she was now rewriting. It had not taken her much to write it back then, mainly because she was used to writing. She had always felt very proud of it, for it had been her longest creation. Not that the length of a story determines its quality, but because she had gone further in her writing than she had ever gone before. She had been able to create a world around the main character, but now that she had reread it several times, she agreed it had not been a very mature writing.

'I still have loads to work on, though. Besides rewriting the end of the story, I now have to update the notes

I took. I need a file to go back to when in doubt about what has happened. That way, every time I reopen the manuscript I won't have to reread everything. That's alright when you've got a couple of pages, but I can't aim for that if I want to write a proper novel,' said Eileen.

'I see that ye're coming to yer senses,' retorted Alick. 'I'm glad ye're realising there's nothing ye need to be taught 'bout writing. Ye've got it within. Anyways, let this old man know how ye plan to do it' he suggested.

'You know how much I like programming Excel sheets, right?'.

'Do ye mean that accounting-friendly, green computer software?' asked Alick. For a man of his age, he was quite good with computers. Since Eileen had moved out to attend university, he had sort of inherited her old desktop computer. It was old and therefore ran quite slowly. But it was useful to him.

'That one, indeed,' said Eileen. 'It can be used for much more than just accounting though. Anyway, what I plan to do is update the table I have already created with more features. If I programme it as I have in mind, I could get quick access to what I need. How do you like that?'.

'This old man doesn' get ye righ' now. Bu' he trusts ye'll show him that table of yers when ye have it,' replied Alick.

Eileen could not find the reason why he wanted to see it, but she nodded her head yes anyway. She had never taken computer lessons herself, so she was not sure she was going to be able to do just what she needed. She had managed to learn things online, and she had been improving a lot since she had started at her new job. A colleague of hers was really good at it, and she had somehow planted the curiosity on her of all the possibilities it offered. In fact, Excel was a software she had rarely used before she had met her, but now that she had used it a little bit more, she was enjoying it a lot. To her, it was as though she was programming, somehow, and she found that solving the problems was as challenging as interesting.

Cleaning up after her, she kissed her grandfather on his forehead as a goodbye and headed upstairs to her room to keep on working.

IV

They kept on looking into each other's eyes alternately, as though by doing that they could figure out what the others were thinking. At the same time however, they were also too afraid to be the first one to present their guesses. After a few hesitant moments, Nora took the lead again and said:

'I despise the idea as much as you do, but the only way to discover what that is,' she said, pointing at Mark's *All Scottish Legends* copy, 'it is by digging into the legends. So…who's in?' she ended up asking, offering her hand to the middle of the circle to make a group shake.

'I…well…I…am curious about what those scrawls are, I can't deny that. But committing to the legends is something serious. I've witnessed what that book is capable of, and I appreciate my life…' said Mark, dubious about joining Nora.

Theresa and Gabe looked from Nora and Mark to each other and, as though a mirror had been placed in between them, they breathed heavily while closing their eyes, joined their hands together to reaffirm one another, and moved them towards the middle of the circle to grip Nora's.

'Oh, come one!' exclaimed Mark, who also extended his hand towards his friends'.

From the moment they had chosen to commit to the legends, they were expectant to what might happen next. Although none of them thought that extraordinary things would start happening the moment all their four hands came into contact. As soon as Mark's hand touched those of Nora, Theresa and Gabe, their respective copies started levitating to stand right in front of their eyes. They could still see each other, but none dared take an eye from the books, for scrawls were being magically doodled on them again.

None of them noticed it, but just as though pulled by an invisible force, all their facial reactions seemed to mirror each others'. The moment they noticed the new scrawls, all their mouths opened to an 'o' shape, that kept growing until they become 'O'-shaped. But that was just the beginning. When their mouths could not grow any bigger, they all screamed. A loud, short yet scaring shout that they had the feeling no one but themselves had been able to hear. And that, on top of that, had somehow made the levitating force stop as suddenly as it had started.

They had only witnessed the potentials of the books the first time they had tried to open them, so they could not be called experts in the matter. Nonetheless, they knew far well that the scrawls were the same for all of them. Although not identical.

'What the f…!' exclaimed Gabe. He could not finish the sentence however, as his sister had nudged him right into his ribs.

'Don't you dare! We weren't taught that way,' said Theresa. Seeing that her brother was about to reply, she added: 'don't Gabe, please! I know this is all very weird, but let's leave swear words for when we grow up. Besides, we've got a lot to deal with, like the fact the books know to whom they belong'.

Nora was as scared as Theresa and the boys. However, the more awkward moments she experienced with the book, the more she focused on trying to understand the whole situation. In the beginning, she had been annoyed at her grandmother for having gifted her something potentially dangerous. Really annoyed actually. But… the more she thought about it, the less annoyed she was starting to feel. She knew her grandmother had always wanted to assure her well-being, so her gifting her that book had to have something hidden that she was not getting at the time being.

'*I don't think granny will ever allow anything dangerous happening to me,*' thought Nora while unconsciously sliding her finger over the new scrawls that had appeared on her copy of the *All Scottish Legends* book. She forced her inner voice to keep repeating that statement however. She needed to reassure herself on that positive belief; she had never been so afraid of reading her name before.

Blinking a tear away from her eyes, she looked up, holding the book still in her hands. She then took a deep breath and tried to randomly open the book on any page other than the protagonists' warning one. She was not surprised the pages were not as unwilling to be open as they had been before her name had been magically signed onto one of them.

'Could you do that again?' suggested Gabe all of a sudden.

'Do what?' asked Nora back, shaking her head as though waking up.

'Flip the pages of your book,' said Theresa. 'Then, look at ours'.

Nora did as suggested, and when she realised that all the books were following her lead, she could not help it and started laughing. It was not a joyful laugh however. It was a deep laugh that she did not recognise as hers, but that she had no control over. The more she flipped the pages, the more she laughed. It kept on for about a minute, until Mark grabbed her from her arm, thus startling her and making the book fall from her hands.

They were all starting to get used to weird things happening when the books were around, so they did not run away, or shout, or do anything that showed how scared they really were. Instead, they all looked at each other, and then, all of a sudden, started laughing. A laugh that lasted until they realised how the books had started vibrating on the ground.

The books kept on vibrating until the last of their laughs were away. And then, all of a sudden, they jumped into the air and started circling in the middle. They came closer and closer until they collapsed, creating a source of light and repulsion power that made them all cover themselves with their hands and lay down. When the force was gone, they uncovered their heads to find that the source of light was still there. In fact, it was so bright that they could not tell what the source of the light was until their eyes got used to the brightness. And when they did discover it, they were all overwhelmed by a cascade of feelings.

And yet again, as suddenly as everything had started, it ended.

'I told you this wasn't a good idea, didn't I?' said Mark, covering his face with both hands. He clearly looked scared.

'We didn't exactly point a gun at you, did we? You joined us because deep down you wanted to, so don't blame us,' replied Gabe, hastily.

'The two of you, that's enough!' said Theresa in an authoritarian voice. 'Besides, I'm not sure any of us had much of an option anyway…'.

Mark and Gabe looked at Theresa as though she had gone completely insane, and when they were about to reply, Nora stood up and took the only book that was now left. The book their four former ones had collapsed into.

'Actually, I do agree with Theresa,' she said, sliding her finger over the spine of the book. From the outside, it looked the same book she had been gifted that very same morning, but deep down she knew it was not. 'I've also got the feeling we were dragged into this unknowingly. It's true we all said we were in, and the moment we confirmed that commitment, the book showed what we needed to know just then: that it accepts us. Nevertheless, I do think this would have happened sooner or later, regardless of whether or not we wanted it to actually happen,' she added, still sliding her finger up and down the spine.

'Oh, so you say! Good! Then why don't you read aloud the legend we were dragged into? Because I assume the book will only let you open it on that page' replied Mark. He was not making any effort whatsoever on not showing his discomfort with how his friends had seemed to constantly disagree with him.

Nora hastily glanced at him. She decided she would not argue with him, or at least not just then. She then opened the book, that indeed would only open on one page:

The legend of Fear monster

By the beginning of the year 1000, just after many people have killed themselves thinking the world would end on December 31st 999, a monster was supposed to have appeared not far from the woodlands that form the natural border between the counties of Highland, Aberdeenshire and Moray, in northern Scotland. Nobody ever saw it, nor they really knew how it looked like. The only proof they had of its existence were some big footprints that were seen around the trees. Those who remained alive accused it of having caused fear to spread around the area and thus started calling it Fear monster.

Afraid of being attacked by it, the inhabitants of the closest settlement decided to build a stone wall all around their houses and fields. They also deemed it necessary to educate their youngest and strongest men on how to fight it, should it be required. But, given that they had never faced anything of the sort, it took them years to try to figure out how it should be done; and by that time, they had nothing to fear, for they never went outside the walls, so they did not see any other footprint.

Such was the case, that generations to come stopped taking it seriously, so they quit getting prepared to face it. No more attacks were attributed to Fear monster, so history became a legend. And the legend then became a tale to educate children.

Five hundred years after it had been named for the first time however, a new attack took place. On a cold winter night in the year 1500, two foreigners dared walk into the forest where the footprints had been seen centuries before. They had reached the area because they were fleeing justice, so they considered hiding in the forest was their best chance for their track to get lost. And for one of them, that was the case altogether.

The inhabitants of the closest settlement, who descended from the ones that had once feared the monster, related feeling dizzy and sleepy for a short period of time, to then find themselves welcoming a fugitive that was claiming for his comrade to have been swallowed by the forest itself. But by then, the legend had become less and less popular, and thus nobody took him seriously. Angry, tired and with no other place to go, he decided to go back to the forest to try and save his mate. None of them was ever seen again.

No more attacks have been reported since then, yet onlookers have visited the area to try to prove the existence of Fear monster. Thus, when big holes were found in the area in 1950, conspiracy theories arose again. Official papers say that the holes were caused by World War II bombing, but the debate is still open, for they did not look like footprints whatsoever. Yet no bomb rests were ever found.

5

'*I never thought I would be able to do this!'* thought Eileen with enthusiasm while switching off her laptop after another productive morning. She had not started working on her new story yet, but she did not care much about it. Even though she still had that new idea coming back and forth in her mind, the more she developed her former red-haired Nora story, the more that unwritten story changed and got procrastinated.

Unlike her grandfather however, she had never seen her full potential. It was not that she did not believe in her capabilities, but rather that she preferred being cautious about airing her whereabouts. So maybe that was the reason she got on so well with Alick. They complimented each other almost perfectly. But, what other option did she have? Her grandparents were the only family she had left.

She was an only child and she had never met her parents. Actually, it had not been until she was nine years old that she had discovered that those she thought were her parents, were in reality her grandparents. And every time she remembered how that day had turned out, she could not stop it and got extremely emotional.

A rainy day after school her grandfather had gone to pick her up, but instead of taking her to her karate practice, he had driven straight home. She had complained about it, but no matter how hard she had tried to convince her grandfather to drive in the opposite direction, he had not done so. And albeit his serious grimace, he had not told her off at all for her misbehaviour.

Once they had gotten home however, she had been unwilling to collaborate, and thus had locked herself from the inside of the car. Every time Alick had unlocked it with his car key, she had locked it again from the inside. That had gone on and on for about half an hour, until Leagsaidh, Eileen's grandmother, had gotten home from work. She had not needed to be told what was going on, as it had been her idea to tell Eileen just then.

Alick had not wanted to tell Eileen until she had grown a little bit older, but he had not found arguments strong enough to make his wife drop the idea. It had been heart-breaking for him having to deal with his grandchild like that, so the moment Leagsaidh arrived, he stepped aside and let her do the talking:

'Eileen, sweethea't,' she had said, knocking on the window car. 'Don't get mad at daddy, it's me who wanted to have a chat with ye'.

'We could've had it after my karate practice!' she had said, tugging her arms in front of her.

'There're things that can't be left fer afte'wards,' had said Leagsaidh, more to herself than to Eileen. 'Please, do come inside the house. The soone' we deal with this, the soone' it'll be ove'. Trust me, Eileen'.

Realising that she was not getting any karate practice that day, she had unfastened her seatbelt, unlocked the car door and stepped outside. She had refused to take her grandmother's hand and had therefore walked by herself from the garage to the front door. Once inside the house, she had left her rainy coat and her wellingtons in the room by the entrance hall. Then, she had headed straight to the dining room, the warmest room in the house. Her grandparents had joined her only a few seconds later.

'So Eileen…trust me, I've tried so many times to do this. I've practised in front of the mirro' so much, that I thought that when the moment arrived, it wouldn't be that ha'd. But I guess I was wrong' had said Leagsaidh, sitting right in front of her grandchild. She had glanced at Alick, grabbed his hand, and resumed talking. 'Ye're a ve'y good young lady, who we love frem the deepest of our hea'ts. We were gifted ye nine yea's ago. That was one of the happiest moments of our lives; only comparable to when our othe' daughter was born'.

Eileen had felt a mixture of feelings ranging from amazement to desolation since her grandfather had driven the opposite direction to the sports centre. She had been only thinking of the karate practise she was missing, but when she had fully comprehended her grandmother's latest statement, her mind had come to the room her body was standing at altogether. For as long as she had known, she did not have any siblings, nor any other relative.

'What are you talking about, mum? I've got no brothers or sisters! It's just you, dad and me'. She had then looked at her grandfather, voicelessly begging him for help.

'What yer mum is trying to say is that…that…'.

'WHAT?' had shouted Eileen, jumping off the chair she had been sitting on. All that nonsense was driving her to her nerves.

'Eileen…,' had whispered Alick. He had barely had any voice to say it aloud. He had never wanted to hide it from her, yet the circumstances had escaped his control. 'What yer mum's trying to say is that she's not really yer mum, but yer grandma. Our othe' daughter was yer mum'.

'Prove that nonsense!' had said Eileen in tears. Out of all the things she could have been told at that moment, that was the last thing she had ever imagined. There had never been any photos in the house of anyone she did not know personally, except for the ones of the parents of her… grandparents. How weird it had been for her to start thinking of Alick and Leagsaidh as her grandparents.

Yet she had refused to believe anything unless she got it proved. Back then she did not know that would determine her future career, but that proving-need had made her become the scientist she had grown up to be. Thus, when Alick had offered his hand to her, she had taken it and had followed his lead. They had walked outside the dining room, passed the living room towards the stairs up until the attic.

Eileen had never been allowed in there. Every time she had asked about the possibility of having a little exploring adventure, as she used to call it, she had been told that there was never anything in attics for children. Thus, when they had reached the third storey and she had realised the intentions of her grandfather, she had known altogether that maybe the only attic that had held things not meant for children had been the one in her household.

Once inside the attic, they had walked past hundreds of cardboard boxes until they had reached a pile that read '*Nora & Aksel*'.

'I'll leave ye he'e to go th'ough it,' had said Alick, taking the box from the top of the pile and leaving it on the ground for Eileen to be able to explore it by herself.

'Don't leave, please,' had pleaded Eileen. 'Stay here with me'.

- V -

When Nora finished reading the legend, she shut the book with a shaking hand. Her face was all pale. She had played her bravest self to stop thinking of dangerous things that could happen to her or her friends. But the fact that weird things kept happening every time they did something with the book was not helping.

'I told you this wasn't a good idea. I TOLD YOU!' shouted Mark, standing up and walking in circles, as though that might help him get his mind cleared.

'For goodness sake, Mark, STOP!' shouted Gabe. 'I've told you already that we didn't point a gun at you. We are as scared as you are, trust me we are. But I'm telling you this' he said, placing himself right in front of Mark and putting both his hands over his friend's collar bones, 'only courage will take us out of this. We have no other option but to look forward and face anything that we might come across. We are all in this, together'.

Nora had only met the boys that very same day. She did not want to argue with them just then, so she had been pleased to Gabe for having calmed Mark down. He was really putting her to her nerves. Although that was nothing compared to how Theresa was feeling.

Leaving the book in between herself and Theresa, she asked her: 'What are your thoughts about it?'.

'I...I don...don't know,' said Theresa, sobbing. Once she could control her breathing, she resumed: 'I've said it before, I don't think we ever had much of an option. I'm really scared about it all, but I trust my granny. Or better said, I want to trust her'.

'I feel you,' said Nora, letting her head rest on Theresa's shoulder.

They remained in that position for a few more minutes, until Nora realised that they had not discovered what Mark's scrawl was. In the beginning, she had been thinking of the reasons as to why her grandmother might have gotten her involved with that, but realising that that mental effort would be worthless unless she asked Mary herself, she had switched to pondering their options with the legend.

The protagonists had been very clear about the book unravelling its information at the due time. So far, they had been able to connect everything together, except for that one scrawl. She was still as clueless about its meaning as she had been before reading the legend.

'Guys,' she said, making both Gabe and Mark come closer to where Theresa and she were sitting, 'have you realised we still don't know what the fourth scrawl means?'.

Given how Mark reacted to her question, Nora realised he had not given that a thought whatsoever. After Gabe had talked him out of his negativity, he had been able to breathe slowly and stop blaming the others for his involvement with the legend. But after he was guided towards that topic again, he started walking and talking nonsense again.

Breathing heavily, Gabe let him do that and decided to stay where he was. Sitting down next to his sister, he said:

'Alike him,' he said, pointing his right thumb backwards, towards where Mark was talking to himself, 'I hadn't. What do you reckon that might be?'.

'The footprints and the forest scrawls are easy to connect with the legend. The musical notes have to be related to the melody that Nora heard coming out of the book. But the fourth scrawl…,' said Theresa, scratching her forehead, 'I've no idea. Could I see it again though?'.

'Indeed,' said Nora, grabbing the book and opening it on the protagonists' warning page.

The three of them looked at the four scrawls once again, wondering why one of them was so difficult to be connected to the story. They had been given the information, so they had the feeling they better knew what it all meant before proceeding any further. If they had been granted the information just then, it was because they needed to make the most out of it just then. Otherwise, they would have not been given anything.

In the meanwhile, Mark kept walking around in circles and talking to himself, not bothered at all about what his friends' whereabouts were. He had been excited about doing some exploring with his friends when his grandmother had given him the book for his birthday, just a month before the arrival of Nora to the village. When he had first grabbed the book, he had had the same urge to be alone with it as the others had described. But his experience with the book had gone beyond.

Alike it had happened to Nora, Theresa and Gabe, his book had also jumped off his hands to open on the protagonists' warning page. He had not been sure at the moment, but ever since he had listened to Nora's experience, he was becoming more and more sure that he had also heard a melody coming from the book. Everything had happened so quick however, that by the time he had realised there was a melody playing, it was over. Nonetheless, he had a strong feeling it was known to him. And, with that idea in mind, he had sat by the desktop and had grabbed the book with trembling hands. It had remained opened the whole time, and because he had not taken an eye from it, he had been able to witness how the page had been magically filled, just like how their names had been doodled onto it.

Yet the others had not described that happening, so that had gotten him thinking. Had that been because he had been the first one to receive the book? Was the book somehow returning to life? Were the scrawls at all connected to the personalities of to whom they belonged? Why had he gotten something that looked like a mountain, or a hill, or a...

'Cave!' he shouted. 'I think that is a cave!'.

'What do you mean you think it's a cave?' asked Gabe, who was containing himself to run over him to shut him up.

'I mean, I'm not sure it's indeed a cave, but it could very well be,' he said, sitting down in between Nora and Gabe. 'I was there thinking when it all came to my mind. I haven't told you, but unlike what had happened to you, when I first opened my copy, I witnessed how the protagonists' warning letter was handwritten by an invisible hand. When the book first jumped off my hands and opened itself on a random page, it was completely blank. It all happened very quickly, but the moment the melody started playing, the page started to be scribbled.

»However, right before the first letter appeared, a line seemed to have been doodled, like marking the margins. I've only just realised that what I saw that day was a bigger version of the scrawl I got afterwards. It seemed to fade away after a few seconds, but now that I come to think about it, it's got the same outline'.

Attentively listening to Mark, the others realised that his suggestion was indeed feasible. That did not make them any less scared, although a small shadow of happiness appeared in their hearts.

'I guess that if we find out whether or not there is a cave hidden in the forest, we'll know where to head to when we wander into it. Have you ever been in there?' asked Theresa, determined to leave her fear behind her.

But they all shook their heads no.

'I guess the only option we've got left is asking our grannies,' said Nora. 'They got us into this, and they won't be unravelling anything from us. We're ninety-nine per cent sure we've got everything right so far. It will be as easy as a yes or no question. Let's go' she added, standing up and putting the only book that they had left inside her backpack to head back to her grandmother's.

Wiping her tears away, Eileen smiled at herself in the mirror that hanged on the back of her room door. Her eyes however were not looking into her reflection, but right into a photo that her grandfather and she had hanged on the wall fifteen years before.

Every time she looked at that photo, she could not help but feel guilty for not missing them. But, how could she? She had never met them in person. They had been long gone before her first memory had been chiselled in her brains.

Closing the door again and turning around, she headed back to place herself right in front of the photo and said: 'I know we've never met, but I hope you're as proud of me as grandpa is. I don't know if I have ever told you, but it took me years to be able to call them grandpa and grandma without having second thoughts. I cried a lot in my room without them knowing. I guess they battled their own demons, but for a nine-year-old girl, it was a really heavy burden to put on her shoulders.

»I did not only have to get used to the idea that those I had always known as my parents were, in reality, my grandparents, but I had to also face meddlesome people. And trust me when I say, these last were the ones that I struggled the most with. From a grown-up's perspective, I now know that I shouldn't have paid them any attention, but back then I didn't know that. Although I guess that made me stronger, somehow' she added, caressing the frame that contained a photo of her parents, Nora and Aksel, happily smiling and holding a sleepy baby girl Eileen.

On their way home, they had agreed that they would put all their apples in the same basket. Their reasoning had been, that they would press whoever they decided to ask more if they were all there. Albeit they had agreed on that, they were having trouble deciding who they should ask first. Somehow, they all wanted their grandmothers to be chosen.

'I reckon my granny should be the chosen one because I was the first one to be handed the book,' said Mark. 'Besides, I think it's fair, given that I was dragged into this by you' he added, turning around and pointing his finger at them all.

'Don't you dare go back there, Mark,' warned him Gabe. 'Anyway, I think we should go to my granny's; at the end of the day, it's also Theresa's grandma, which means she's related to two of us…'.

Theresa looked from her brother to Nora, wishing that he would shut up. It was true he had talked Mark out of his stubbornness, or at least he had tried to. But she did not agree with him on the fact that they should go to their grandmother's just because she was related to two of them. After all, it had been Nora who had taken the lead and decided to ask the elderlies. Besides, she had had the feeling that the books had not just randomly collapsed into one, but that they had all collapsed into Nora's.

But she did not know how to tell the boys. It was just a feeling she had had, even though she was positive Nora might have appreciated that as well. Thus, shifting gears somehow, she decided to voice her thoughts:

'You're right, Gabe…'.

'But…,' said Gabe, realising that her sister was not done.

'But I think we should go to Mary's,' she said, all at once. 'If I recall it properly, I think grandma said that it had been her idea, so the least we can do is ask her the questions we deem necessary. What's more, you probably haven't noticed, but the only book we have left is Nora's,' she added, taking her hands out of her pockets and pointing at Nora's backpack.

From how the boys reacted, it was clear that they had not paid attention to that detail. It was insignificant for sure, but given what they had gotten themselves involved with, even the most trivial aspects could play a determining role. On the contrary however, Nora had indeed considered that what Theresa was suggesting could actually be true.

The moment she had held the book after the collision, she had had the feeling she was holding her own's, even though there were no other books left. But she had been clueless about why she had felt that way regarding the book. Unlike what the boys were thinking, she was as scared as them, despite her taking the leading role.

'What gives you that impression, Theresa?' asked Mark after having pondered her statement for a few seconds.

'When we had a closer look at the book while you were talking nonsense, I noticed that all our scrawls,' she said, pointing at him, Gabe and herself, 'were fainter than Nora's. In the beginning, I didn't think it mattered at all, but now that I come to think about it, it is as though the book has chosen her as the leader. All our books followed her lead when she flipped the pages on hers, for instance. That might not be it, but I might as well be right'.

'I see where you are going. But… why me?' asked Nora. The other three startled when she broke her silence. She had been so absent-minded, that they thought she was not listening whatsoever.

Lending a hand to his sister, Gabe replied for her: 'I reckon the book might have recognised your leadership attitude. I don't know'.

Nodding her head yes, Theresa glanced apologetically at Nora, who was feeling overwhelmed. She was finding it hard to believe that the surprises her grandmother had kept for her included the latest events she had gone through. To her, it all seemed to have been extracted from a science fiction movie, or something of the sort.

Hence, after that dubious moment, they decided to go to Mary's. And, when they arrived, they were not impressed by the fact that all their grandmothers were awaiting them there. They were getting quite used to unusual things happening.

Once inside the house, all of them silently followed Mary to the living room, where the table had been set up for supper. There were seven chairs placed around the round wooden table that Nora's grandfather had handcrafted soon after he had married Mary. As valuable as it sentimentally was, it was only used for special occasions, so Nora could not help but put on a face when she saw the feast that laid right in front of her eyes. After all, they were not but to discuss about a rare old book.

'Have a seat, please,' said Mary, turning around when she reached the door frame from the living room. 'We shall enjoy this supper together. And fear not, we will answer your questions on the due time'.

The teenagers alternately looked at one another. Neither of them had voiced what they were up to, yet their grandmothers seemed to have known altogether. Naturally, none of them could hide their surprised grimaces, although they were not as they would have been should they had not experienced anything weird before. But that was not their case. Sadly for them, they were becoming used to getting more questions than answers as they discovered new things related to the legends book.

'I know you have been awaiting this moment since you left the park,' said Mary. 'Oh, why those faces? I'm not a witch or anything of the sort, but you boys, and girls' she added, leaning her head towards Nora and Theresa, who were now sitting on the couch, side by side, 'have fresh green signs on your trousers. Anyway, without further ado, let's get ourselves into what you came here for: the book. What have you experienced so far?'.

'What do you mean what have we experienced *so far*?' said Nora, really emphasizing the last two words.

'Do you really ever thought we would get you involved in anything that would represent a real threat to your lives?' said Abby, standing up from her chair to turn it around to sit face to face with them.

'Granny!' exclaimed Mark, who could not believe his grandmother knew the book had extraordinary properties.

Abby tenderly looked at his grandchild, to then continue talking as she had not been interrupted: 'We are aware of how the book behaves when handled by the right persons. It is an extraordinary book because you are all extraordinary people'.

'For Goodness sake, Abby!' exclaimed Gabe. 'I know how our grandmothers would think of us as extraordinary, good-looking and smart teenagers. Do tell us something we don't know, thanks'.

'You'll do best shutting up, boy,' said Mary. 'Ooh, don't play so alarmed. Swear wording was invented long before we were born' she added, pointing at her colleagues.

Noticing the bewilderment growing inside the teenagers, she resumed: 'You came here for answers, and answers you will get. However, we shall ask you to not interrupt us at any point. You will only talk when directly summoned to do so. Is that understood?.

'Understood,' said the four of them in unison.

7

That frame had been hanging on the wall for fifteen years, and she had caressed it more than once before, so the fact it fell as soon as she touched it made her startle. Eileen's heart started racing as though she had been running non-stop for hours, for she thought she had broken the frame that contained one of the few memories she had from her parents.

With a shaking hand, she grabbed the frame and turned it around, to find the same smiley faces that had always been on it. The glass covering the photo looked as smooth as it had always looked. Kissing it softly, she kneeled again to be able to reach the hanger, but she suddenly felt a prick on her right knee, which made her jump and let the frame fly off her hands.

Worried by the sound the frame had done when it had hit the wall, she stood up and jumped over it. She did not doubt that it was broken now. Cursing herself for her blunder, she started cleaning the mess up. Once no big glass fragments were left on the floor, she headed to the door to go grab a broom and a dustpan, but she kept still when she looked into her reflection and realised she was bleeding on her knee. Losing sight of her reflection, and glancing at her right knee, Eileen realised that there was a thumbtack stuck to her trousers.

'*Where did this come from?*' she asked herself while putting up the leg of her trousers to see how deep the wound was.

She did not have anything hammered on top of her bed, except for the frame that contained the first photo she had ever been taken with both her parents. But the hanger was where it had always been, so she realised that the thumbtack might have been attached to the back of the frame. Thus, forgetting about the broom and the dustpan, and even about healing her wound, she turned around and went directly to her desktop. She grabbed what was remaining of the frame and turned it around to find three thumbtacks indeed attached to its back, and a hole that unquestionably suggested that there had once been a fourth one.

When she had first discovered that frame in the box in the attic, it already contained the photo, so she had not considered the possibility of changing it to a newer and more stylish one. All she had cared about was that it was the proof that her grandparents had not lied to her on the fact that they were indeed her grandparents.

Out of all the photos that were in the box, she had chosen that one to be the one that would be on her wall forever, so she had forgotten about the thumbtacks altogether. If she had at all realised they were there. Accepting they were useless given the current status of the frame, she unstuck them all. And once she did, a small piece of paper fell over the desk, together with the photo. It was handwritten, but she did not recognise the lettering:

Liebe Nora,

Vielen Dank für das Foto. Ihr seht sehr glücklich darauf aus. Ich werde einen besonderen Platz dafür finden. Bitte besuchen Sie uns bald wieder.

Deine Klara.

She was keen on languages, so she was able to understand what the small letter read without having to go to Google translator for a clumsy translation. What she was not so happy about was the fact that she had never heard a word about someone named Klara who was friends with her parents. She had been answered every single question she had ever asked about the whereabouts of Nora and Aksel, yet she had the feeling that name had never shown up.

With galloping questions to her head, she grabbed the photo and the small letter and headed downstairs to the living room, where her grandfather was sitting in front of her old computer, reading the last chapters she had emailed him.

'Aren't ye a bit early fer lunch?' asked Alick when he realised Eileen was standing right behind him.

'I'm not hungry, or at least not foodwise,' said Eileen. ' Have you got any idea who Klara is though?' she added, leaving both the photo and the letter on top of the keyboard.

Eileen had taught herself to tell when someone was lying, just by seeing how they reacted when seeing something for the first time. And by the look on her grandfather's face, she could tell that he had no idea who that person was, so she was not surprised when he said he did not know her.

'What does the lette' say? Which language is it w'itten on anyway?' he asked, giving it back to Eileen. She did not need it, as the words had been chiselled to her head. But she took it anyway.

'It's German, grandpa,' said Eileen. 'And it says: Dear Nora, thank you so much for the photo. You look so happy on it. I will find a special place for it. Please, do come visit sometime. See you soon, Klara.

»Do you reckon grandma might know who this Klara is?'.

'I don' know. But we shall give it a t'y,' he said, turning around to close all the windows on the computer before turning it off. Once done, they went to the kitchen, where Leagsaidh was watching TV.

'Hi grandma,' greeted Eileen. 'Grandpa and I were wondering whether you knew someone named Klara, with a k. All the hints we can give you is that she's German-speaking and that she knew my parents' she added, handing the letter to her.

And the moment Leagsaidh took the letter in her hands, Eileen could tell that she did indeed recognise the lettering. Her reaction had been so different to that of Alick's. Her eyes showed differently, and her hands were shaky. She knew who that Klara was, and she had been caught red-handed.

'I don' know this Klara, but the Clarissa she was born,' said Leagsaidh. 'She was my sister'.

- VII -

Nora had never seen her grandmother behaving that way. The only person she had ever seen her raising her voice to had been her parents, and she reckoned that was normal somehow, given the family ties they shared. At the end of the day, one is the bravest and the hardest when confronting loved ones. But how dared she direct like that to someone she was not related to, she could not understand. And her wording! She was old enough as to know that most people used swear words at some point every day, but she had never heard those words coming from her grandmother's mouth.

And like it had happened to her when she had met Mark, she was unable to hide her bewilderment. She knew there was not but confusion on her face; and the more she tried to hide it, the more apparent it became. She did not need a mirror to look into her reflection to know that: the look of others seeing her was hard enough.

'Nora, sweetheart' said Mary, coming closer to her, 'you too don't play so alarmed, will y…?'.

'How dare you?' interrupted Mark. 'Have you listened to yourself? It looks as though you have been brainwashed or something. You don't seem to be the same person I came to this evening' he added, tinging his words with the bravery he did not feel.

'Haven't I said that you are only to talk when summoned to do so?' asked Mary, leaning her head towards Mark's. 'I haven't changed a bit since you left my house earlier today. But we are talking about serious stuff, and to do so, we have to set some rules. I'm afraid that given the circumstances, you can't be left aside, but you'll do well keeping that big mouth of yours close the longer, the better.

»Anyway, I reckon you all have realised by now that you are involved with something greater than us. We might be able to give you some recommendations, but don't expect us to guide you throughout the whole process; we are simply not allowed to do so. Thus, give us a heads-up, how much do you know so far?'.

As taken aback as she was, Nora was completely unable to produce any coherent sound. All she could produce were unintelligible babbles, so Theresa took over her and told the elderlies what they knew. She briefly summarised their first experiences with the books, to then tell them how the books had been brought into the air by an unknown force. She also mentioned how their names had been magically doodled at the end of the protagonists' warning page, and how they had all followed Nora's when she had flipped the pages on hers.

'And then, all of a sudden, they started vibrating and ended up collapsing into just one book,' she said, holding tight to her brother's hand to find some comfort.

'Indeed,' said Abby, looking unsurprised by the extraordinary story she had just been retold. 'You have mentioned there were scrawls in your former books. What were they? Are they still present in the collapsed book?'.

'Oh yes, they are still there. As for what they are…I got some footprints, which will undoubtedly be a representation of Fear monster's, if it exists at all,' said Theresa, challenging the elderlies with that last comment. Seeing how they did not react whatsoever, she decided it was better to keep on listing the scrawls. 'Gabe got some trees, which we reckon is the forest that is mentioned in the legend. Nora got some musical notes, which might be because of the melody that she heard coming out of her copy the first time she opened it. And Mark… well, we are not one hundred per cent sure as the scrawl could mean different things, but we think he got a cave. Should that be the case then, it must be Fear monster's dwelling'.

Clap, clap, clap.

'Very well, very well indeed,' sardonically said Mary while still clapping at the teenagers. 'You have unravelled the obvious which, you know, is a good start. I don't like however that scepticism in your voice. You talk of Fear monster as though you didn't believe it existed, am I wrong? Haven't you witnessed what that book is capable of? Are you really telling me you don't believe in legends?'.

That last question Mary had formulated took the four teenagers by surprise. It had been long since they were last impressed by fairy-tales, and even though legends were not strictly all made up, there was a huge difference between believing everything was real, or just some bits. Nevertheless, they had all witnessed more than once that that book was not an ordinary one.

'Grandma…?' said Nora with a shaky voice. 'Are you seriously telling us that we must believe everything? Literally everything that appears in that book? Are you suggesting that it is not a legends book, but a history book?'.

'Oh deary, I know it is hard to believe it just now, but yes, you are to do as the book says,' said Mary, recovering her tender voice. 'Although I guess you aren't surprised if I say we aren't allowed to say much more. You'll discover things on the due time because…'.

'Knowing too much is sometimes as dangerous as knowing too little' the three elderlies said in unison.

The fact that they all knew the last sentence of the protagonists' warning letter did not take Nora by surprise. Other things were keeping her mind busy, like the fact that her grandmother had just asked her and her friends to do as an old book with apparently magical powers wished. Knowing a sentence from a book was the least scary act that Nora had witnessed since they had finished supper.

'But you haven't said anything at all!' shouted Gabe, letting go of his sister's hand and standing up. 'You have played your roles very well, but there's nothing you've said that gives us a heads-up of what you have gotten us involved into. If you expect me to do as told, then you'll have to give me reasons as to why I should do that. I'm not a five-year-old anymore. I won't do as I'm told just because of the fact I'm told to do so,' he added, firmly crossing his arms in front of him.

'Yeah, neither will I,' said Mark, imitating his friend and also standing up.

Both Gabe and Mark turned to look at Theresa and Nora, and just a look was enough for them to stand up and also say: 'Nor we'.

And, unlike the teenagers had expected after their firm reaction to the nonsense they had been told, instead of a glimpse of concern in the faces of their grandmothers, what they saw really worried them. Their looks had become something between amused and bewildered, which to them made no sense whatsoever. How could they find the situation any hilarious? The legend talked about disappearances, and they had suggested everything that was written in the book had indeed happened! There was much more to it that they were not sharing, whatever the reason they had decided not to do so was.

Out of all of them however, the one who seemed to be the most upset was Nora. She thought she knew her grandmother really well, especially after their bond had grown together because of their letters. But the latest events had shown her, that she did not know her that well. And that feeling was heart-breaking. She could not feel anger, or horror, or hopelessness. All she could feel was a deep pain right in her chest. A pain that, she knew, no painkiller would be able to fade away.

8

Out of all the things that had come to Eileen's head as to who that Klara might be, that was the latest she had thought about. If she had at all even considered that possibility. She thought that might be a relative of her father's, or the landlord her mother had had when she had lived in Germany, or even a neighbour, but her great aunt? That was the hardest one to believe, yet it was apparently the only one that was real.

Although the confusion that Eileen felt was nothing compared to how Alick was feeling. He had never heard of his wife having had a sister. Thus, when Eileen peered at her grandfather and saw his soul reflected on his face, she felt a twist on her heart that was only comparable to that one moment fifteen years before.

Breathing slowly, she closed her eyes and started counting backwards. She needed to relax a bit and let the anger fade away before addressing her grandmother again. After a few minutes, she reopened her eyes and said: 'Explain yourself, please'.

Leagsaidh had known from the moment she had set her eyes on the letter that she had no other option than to explain everything to them. Regardless of the scary feeling that she had had her whole life about having to face that moment, she had kept on practising in front of the mirror just in case. That technique had proved useless when she had told her grandchild the truth about her parents, but that had been the only way she had found to keep her soul steady. As much as she wanted to forget all about her sister, recurrent memories kept coming back to her, especially at night-time.

'I'm…I'm so''y,' said Leagsaidh, bursting into tears. 'I…I…'.

'Leagsaidh. Do it when ye're ready. We aren't going anywhere,' said Alick. Standing up, he put the kettle on and searched for a teabag. As heartbroken as he felt, love was still a more powerful feeling inside him. There were no rancour or snub tilts on his voice; he seemed as loving as ever. But Eileen could tell he had also felt a deep pain in his chest.

A pain that only words could heal.

Once the water was ready, Alick poured it on the mug he had prepared with the tea bag and offered it to his wife. When she grabbed it, he kissed her on the forehead and left the kitchen. After a few seconds, Eileen followed him. She was not sure how she was supposed to feel about her grandmother. She had the impression that she had the right to be angry at her for having hidden that part of her past from her. After all, fifteen years before she had promised there were no more hiding information from one another. But she also felt sorry. Up to that moment, she was uncertain as to whether Klara was still alive; yet the fact that she had said that she did not know Klara, but the Clarissa she had been born, suggested that their relationship had been since long broken.

'Will ye forgive me, Eileen?' asked Leagsaidh just when Eileen was under the door frame. Turning around and holding up her tears, she nodded her head yes.

Turning around again, Eileen let the tears flow all over her face. She had played strong in front of her grandmother because she realised she was going through enough. But the moment she knew she was not been seeing, she could not hold them any longer. And like it had happened fifteen years before, she realised it would take her a long time to be able to trust her grandmother again, if she were ever able to do it at all again.

Wiping her tears up with the back of her sleeve, she entered the living room. She knew her grandfather would be there, and even though she did not feel like talking at the moment, she wanted to be accompanied. Thus, she let herself fall on her favourite spot: the armchair by the fireplace. Once done, she took her slippers off, curled herself in a foetus-like way, and closed her eyes. She did not think she would fall asleep given the latest circumstances, but she eventually did. And when she opened her eyes again, she could tell a few hours had passed.

'What time is it?' she asked, stretching out. Her whole body hurt, although it was nothing compared to the deep pain that she still felt on her chest.

'Passed half-past five,' said Alick. 'Ye we'e so deeply asleep, that I wouldn't dare waking ye up. Dinner is on the fridge. Go eat something, I can hear yer guts frem he'e'.

Eileen wanted to protest, but her guts roared again, which made her lose any credibility. However, she deemed convenient to be well nourished before facing whatever it was that her grandmother had to tell her. Thus, stretching out one last time, she put on her slippers and headed to the kitchen. Her grandmother was still there. She looked sad and sorry. It had been a lot of hours since she had left the kitchen that morning, but Eileen had the impression that neither of her grandparents had moved except for the basic human necessities. She muttered an almost inaudible *hello* to Leagsaidh, and went straight to the fridge. Her guts were roaring like crazy.

When she opened the refrigerator, she found two glass lunch boxes with leftovers. Without opening the lids, she figured out that her grandparents had not had dinner together, and that her dinner was to be made out of both of them. The atmosphere was disturbed enough to make her dinner choice be the spark to start yet another riot.

She served her meal and ate as slowly as she could. Even though her guts were claiming to be filled, she did not feel like eating whatsoever. All she wanted was for their chat to be over so that she would be able to start the healing process of her deep heart pain. Given her past experience, she had a heads-up onto what she would feel once she found out the truth. But that did not mean she wanted to go through that again. Not when it had been the same person who had caused it twice.

Once done, she did her dishes and cleaned after herself, before addressing her grandmother: 'I think the moment has arrived, grandma. Shall we join grandpa in the living room?'.

All she got for an answer was a sad stare from Leagsaidh while she stood up from the chair she had been sitting on. The slowness she did it with demonstrated she had indeed been sitting on it for longer than she ever did. Grinning and bearing it, Eileen retraced her steps and helped her out.

'Grab my arm, grandma' she said, offering her right arm for Leagsaidh to grab it. Once she did, they both slowly walked to the living room, where Alick was still sitting, waiting for them.

Eileen helped Leagsaidh get comfortable, and then she sat on her favourite armchair. Letting her slippers fall from her feet, she acquired the foetus-like position again and waited for her grandmother to start her relating.

'I don't know whe'e to start frem,' said Leagsaidh, clearing her throat. 'Me practising in front of the mirror all these yea's is again proving completely useless, so I will just rustle up.

»The fi'st thing I do want to tell ye though, is that I am really so''y. I neve' meant fer this to grow this big. I know it was all in my hands, and that it wouldn't have been that big of an issue, should have I told ye befo'e, but ye should understand as well that I neve' meant to hu't ye.

»So... yes, Klara, or Clarissa, is my sister. My twin sister in fact. As twins, we were ve'y close growing up. We knew eve'ything frem one another. We had an older brothe' called Bhaltair, but our relationship with him was neve' that close. We loved him, and he loved us back, yet we were neve' ve'y sentimental with him. He was ve'y old-schooled, and frequently did not approve of our ground-breaking behaviou'. Back then, women were only raised to be at home, to wait fer their beloved husbands to retu'n home frem work to find a clean house and a meal ready to eat. But neithe' Clarissa nor me shared that mindset. We wanted to explore the world and live thousands of adventures. We even wrote up a contract!' added Leagsaidh, pulling out a paper from her apron's pocket. Handing it to Eileen, she resumed: 'We wrote that up a couple of years before World War II started. The tension had neve' really left after World War I, or so Bhaltair said. He was a soldier in the army, and because we were only teenagers, and females, we were neve' allowed on his reunions with our father. Yet we managed to find out things.

»And that's when Clarissa started changing. All of a sudden, we weren't that close anymo'e. She started keeping secrets frem me. She misbehaved in the house, and dared to answer back our father and Bhaltair. That gained her loads of grounding, but that didn't seem to be any effective. After eve'y punishment, she came out yet mo'e rebellious. She was a ve'y cleve' girl, so at the beginning, I didn't really pay much attention to the fact she was always talking about the war and how she didn't understand how Britain dared face Germany. She even started learning German, and that was also the time when she changed her name to Klara.

»I can't deny I was hurt by the sudden turn of events. I had other girl friends who were also changing their behaviours, mainly due to their brothers, fathers and lovers being sent to war. Undoubtfully, our brother Bhaltair was sent to the front a few months after the beginning of the war; and even our father was called on list. He had never been in the army, yet the government claimed all men in the nation were to be ready to defend Britain. Men, and only men. That made Clarissa really angry. She indeed disapproved of our country battling against her beloved Germany, wherever her sudden interest in that country had come frem, but I think what made her the most angry was that women were left behind. As though we couldn't be brave, or strong, or smart. As though we were nothing more than a puppet to serve a man's wishes.

»With our brother gone, the ground-breaking behaviou' of Clarissa grew to limits beyond our father's patience. She was skipping her duties and, eve'y time she was told off, she talked back in German, knowing how much we both loathed that. And don't take me wrong; it wasn't because our country was battling Germany, it was because none of us spoke a word of German. We didn't know what she was saying, although something told us she wasn't being kind at all. The question that I kept asking myself all the time, was how she had learned German so fast. As I've said, she was a sma't girl, but let me remind you that back then there were no TV or internet. So she had to have contact with a German native.

»It took me a while to discove' who she was having contact with, and when I found out, I didn't know what to do. I knew I couldn't contact Bhaltair, and telling father wasn't something I wanted to do. Not afte' he had been listed to go to the front. I tried to talk her out of it, to convince her that that German boy she was seeing was no good fer her, but she wouldn't listen.

»The night before our father was meant to leave to the front, they had a huge argument. As I've said, her misbehaviou' was reaching its limits, and when father told her to settle her head and be with me to take care of the cattle, she said that she wouldn't waste her lifetime with me, when she could be with her beloved Leon. I was eavesdropping from the kitchen, as their shouts had become so loud that no matte' how hard I tried, I still heard what they were yelling at each other. And trust me, that comment broke my hea't. After all we had gone through, after all we were to go through, she had chosen that Leon over me.

»Clarissa left that same night, and I never saw her again. My father departed the following morning, and I never saw him again either. It was only a couple of weeks after he had left to the front that I learned of his passing. We only got to bury him because of Bhaltair; he managed to discover he had been killed and did eve'ything in his power to find his body and take it back home. I was devastated. I had gone through that painful trance when our mother had died because of the Spanish flu, but that time it was even worse, fer I was by myself. It's true I had Bhaltair by my side during the burial, but it was twice as painful because my significant half wasn't with me. And also because I had to deal with Bhaltair going crazy when I told him eve'ything that had happened. He asked me to contact our sister for her to apologize, and that I tried. It took me a while to find her whereabouts. Apparently, she'd left to Germany with that Leon. I couldn't contact her because I didn't have any address to do so, thus I decided to wait until Bhaltair would be back frem war. But he never came back. He was also killed on the front. Unfortunately, I wasn't able to bury him, so the grieving process took a while.

»I neve' received a letter frem Clarissa asking how our father and brother were, asking whether or not they had returned home frem war at all. I kept my faith up longer than my friends thought I would. But after some time, faith turned into rancour, rancour into hatred, and hatred into callousness.

»And that's why I've never mentioned a single word about Clarissa. Because fer me, she's as dead as my father and Bhaltair'.

- VIII -

Silence took over the room. The pain in Nora's heart was still very strong, that much in fact that she did not dare ask anything else. She had been told enough nonsense for a night. Besides, she had the impression that none of the elderlies would be sharing anything else that would help them, so she decided to head to her room. She even did not say goodbye when she left. She could not think about anything else but how much her grandmother had hurt her, so she did not notice how Theresa, Gabe and Mark silently followed her to her room. They felt the need to be together to support one another.

'We'll stay here with you, Nora. We aren't going anywhere,' said Theresa when they reached Nora's bedroom door.

Nora blinked repeatedly to hold her tears before turning around, but it was useless. The moment she stared at her friends, she could not play strong anymore. She burst into tears while hugging them all. She sounded so sad that the other three ended up bursting into tears as well.

Not even today can they recall how much time that crying hug lasted. What they do know however is that that hug created a bond between them as no other circumstance would have. Once they were done, which could have been two to ten minutes later than they had interlaced their arms, they went inside the room.

'Thank you so much for staying around,' said Nora, wiping her tears with the back of her sleeve. 'I don't have mattresses for us all though. How do you reckon we're going to sleep?' she ended up asking while letting herself fall on her bed.

'I don't think I'll get much sleep anyway, so I could just lie on the carpet. Two blankets will do,' said Mark, imitating Nora.

'Same here,' said Gabe, also letting his body rest over the bed.

'That's very sweet of you, but we do need some rest' said Theresa, closing the door behind them. 'If we are to explore, which we are, we need to be fully rested before heading to the forest. We will otherwise not have our full capacities'.

'How do you reckon we could do that?' asked Gabe to his sister. 'I mean, I know you are trying to be sensible here, but it's not because I want to fall asleep that I actually will. It doesn't work like that'.

'If you relax you might eventually fall asleep. And trust me, I think that's our best chance,' she said. Seeing how her brother was about to reply, she silenced him with a flip of her hand and continued talking: 'I know the chat with our grannies hasn't been as productive as we wished it had been, but we have to try and see what we can get from it. They might have said something that has gone unseen...'.

'All I can recall is I was told off for talking when not summoned to do so,' said Mark, sitting up. He sounded really annoyed.

Although it seemed as though Nora was not there, she was silently listening to what her friends were saying. After her bitterness had slightly faded away, she was, like Theresa, trying to see whether they had been shed some light to their current situation. There must have been something that their grandmothers had said that could be of some use when they eventually penetrated the forest...

'You know what, I guess that part is actually quite important,' said Nora. 'We not talking when not asked to do so, I mean. My grannie got very serious about that. I have never seen her using that wording before. I guess what she wanted us to realise, is that we are not to be impertinent. We clearly don't know what we are getting ourselves involved with, but I've got the feeling they do. They were completely unsurprised when Theresa related our experiences with the book, and they got really crossed when she suggested Fear monster wasn't but a book character. And if I'm honest with you, that's not the reaction I would expect of someone who hasn't experienced this nonsense'.

Before Nora finished talking, Mark felt the urge to reply, but he closed his mouth once she was done. He had been really pissed off by the fact he had been told off for no apparent reason, but listening to what Nora had said, he realised she was probably right. He refused to believe that was the only bit that was useful of the whole gathering, although he had to agree that they had truly not said much.

'Well, they said we got the meaning of our scrawls right. I guess we could praise ourselves for that,' said Theresa. 'At the end of the day, sometimes what lays right underneath one's nose is the thing one sees last'.

'Are you possibly suggesting that that damn book is a history book? Are you also telling us to believe it unquestionably?' asked Mark, once and for all.

'I guess so, yes,' said Theresa, firmly. 'You've witnessed what that book is capable of. I was never a very fairy-tale-impressed type of girl, but I believe that everything that book has done, could only be achieved through magic. I know it seems nonsense to you, it does to me as well, but it's the only explanation I can find as to what has happened. Besides, you know there is always some truth in legends. I wouldn't like to end up as those foreigners that are mentioned in the book, but I guess we have no other choice but to move forward. I am exploring tomorrow. Is anybody coming?' she ended up asking. She was forcing herself to look braver than she was actually feeling, for she had had the impression that no matter how hard they tried to avoid the exploring, it was already too late.

'I guess Theresa is right. My grandma said *I'm afraid that given the circumstances, you can't be left aside,*' said Nora, imitating her grandmother's voice. 'And there's the fact that the books knew to whom they belonged. Our only fate is to do as the book says. I'm in' she added, offering her hand for the others to grab it for a group shake, just like they had done earlier in the park.

Theresa rapidly joined Nora in her initiative and grabbed her hand firmly. Mark and Gabe looked at each other and then nodded while also offering their hands for the group shake.

And, like it had happened when they had agreed to open the book to discover what Mark's scrawl was, the moment their four hands established a direct contact, a sudden force was created from within the book. But because it was still inside Nora's backpack, the vibration it was producing was not enough to unzip the zip fastener, which was somehow making the book increase on its attempts to be set free. Nora let her hand go off the group shake, and jumped on her backpack to take the book herself. Once it was able to come out of the backpack however, the book jumped into the air and started twisting until Nora sat back at her former spot in the circle.

And then, as suddenly as the book had started moving by itself, it stopped. It collapsed and opened on the protagonists' warning letter. It looked as it had looked the last time they had seen it. Yet they all had the feeling that that had not been it. They were waiting for something else to happen, which indeed occurred only a couple of seconds later.

They were still staring at the book, not daring to move until it was done, when the page containing the protagonists' warning letter turned to show the following two blank pages.

As soon as the left page laid completely flat over its previous one, they witnessed how the blank pages were filled again by an invisible hand:

Dear dauntless readers,

We are very happy to welcome you to our story. And please, do forgive us, should we have scared you off. That was never our intention. We simply wanted to prove to you that magic does exist. Not all legends in this book have a magical background, but the one you are getting involved with does. And as such, we needed to be impressive in order to bring that belief back to your teenage brains.

We are aware you have tried to get answers before we provide them to you. We understand the need you feel right now, but we do ask you not to do that again. We won't be that amenable next time.

But enough with the reprimand for the meantime. Let's focus on what is to come.

We told you that we would let you know things on the due time, and the time for the first revelation has indeed arrived. The four of you have agreed to commit to the legend and do the exploring it requires. You have successfully unravelled the meanings of the scrawls (See? We keep our word), so now you must be provided with a map that will guide you through the forest until the very entrance of the cave. Yet fear not, it will be easy to follow. No compass nor great astronomy knowledge are required to follow it. Should you behave properly, it will guide you straight to the entrance of the cave. Should you not, well, we guess neither of you wants to find that out.

Yours sincerely,

The protagonists.

9

Eileen did not know how to feel about what Leagsaidh had just shared with them. It was for sure a very sad story. She felt really sorry for everything her grandmother had had to go through. She herself had not had an easy life, but she had to agree that her grandmother's had been more difficult. She had lost everyone she ever loved at such a young age, that no wonder she never talked about her family. She did have however a photo of her parents, but even though it was on display, it was in a room that guests were never allowed to. Avoiding uncomfortable questions had been her way to protect herself.

She looked from her grandmother to her grandfather and then back again to her grandmother. Alick seemed to be so overwhelmed by the whole situation, that he was completely unable to speak. As for Leagsaidh, she could not say anything else either. She was so impressed by how much her grandmother had been able to say without bursting into tears, that she had felt herself the callousness for Clarissa that her grandmother had described before. But still, the fact that she had kept that contract they had signed when they were only teenagers made Eileen think that she had not forgotten her completely.

We, Clarissa Boyd and Leagsaidh Boyd, declare that we have agreed to break the established rules for women by achieving the following:

1. We will live thousands of adventures. Scotland has enough to offer to beginners, but then we shall travel overseas.

2. *We will travel outside Britain and come back wiser. We shall learn new cooking and new languages.*
3. *We shall only marry on true love. We will not take a man as a husband otherwise.*
4. *We will only have children when we have accomplished all of the above.*

Scotland, 1937.

Clarissa & Leagsaidh.

Eileen had avoided reading the contract when her grandmother had handed it to her before. She had been so immersed in her relating, that she had left it laying on her lap the whole time. The lettering was very flourished yet neat, but knowing the story behind it, she could see the resemblance between that one and the one signed by Klara. They had indeed been written by the same person, however she wanted to be referred to.

After her long sleep, Eileen was not feeling tired whatsoever. Besides, the latest events made her think that her grandparents would not be able to get much sleep either, so she decided to make the most of the fact that her grandmother was willing to talk, and thus dared to ask her: 'How come you kept this anyway?'.

'I wanted to forget the person she had become, but not the one I knew,' said Leaghsaidh, matter-of-factly. 'It's true that ever since she did what she did, I promised meself to never talk 'bout her to anyone, but that doesn't mean I forgot of our past together. It's not because ye want to forget someone, or something, that ye can do it'.

'I…get it, I guess,' said Eileen, trying not to sound doubtful. 'And did you ever try to contact her? After the war ended, I mean'.

'Things were much more complicated back then, deary. If one wanted to be left alone, it was as easy as not telling anyone where ye were heading to. I was lucky I could find out she had left with that Leon. Where to? I don't know. I assume they went to Germany, or even Switzerland'.

'Did you ever meet Leon?'.

'Not personally, no. I only saw him a couple of times befo'e they left the village. No-one really eve' knew how or why he came to Scotland. I'm not sure how old he was eithe', although he looked older than us. Trust me, I've also asked meself a lot of questions about how Clarissa got involved with someone like him'.

'And how come grandpa never heard of her before either? I mean, you can keep to yourself whatever you don't want to share, but people talk' said Eileen, trying with all her will to understand the situation.

'There are times that societies agree not to talk of some things. Eve'ybody knew that I had lost both my father and my brother on the front, so they assumed that I wouldn't like remembering such a painful time. It took me a really long time to be able to smile or laugh again. Luckily fer me though, not many people knew of Clarissa's whereabouts. Because she knew she was doing something that our father wouldn't agree on, she kept it a secret. I think that was the only amenable gesture she eve' had with our family,' added Leagsaidh, holding her rancour. Just by the look she had in her eyes, one could tell that she was not fond of her sister.

Eileen wanted to keep asking her grandmother questions, but she knew she had to be very cautious as to how she should formulate them. It was true that Leagsaidh had been as willing to collaborate as she had been fifteen years before, but she did not want to upset her. Nevertheless, there was one last question that she needed to ask: 'And how come, after all those years, my mum and she got in contact?'.

'I guess ye can call it destiny,' said Leagsaidh, while looking for something in her apron's pocket. Pulling out what looked like a letter, she said: 'But ye might wanna hear it frem yer mum. This is the letter she wrote to me when she first met her'.

The four teenagers read the protagonists' new letter in silence. They were getting used to the fact the book could communicate with them as the protagonists wished. But that did not mean that every time it did so, they did not get really scared all about it. Truth must be told however, their fear was not reaching the same level every time.

After they had assimilated the information they had been provided with, they agreed to try and get some sleep before heading to the woods the next morning. They had not been told much, yet that was all they were going to get before starting their adventure.

They managed to find some extra blankets stored in Nora's room cupboards. Her friends did not know that those had not been there before, but she was feeling so tired that she let it go. It could have very well been an idea of her grandmother's.

When they turned off the lights, they all tried to sleep. Sadly, neither of them was able to get more than just a couple of hours of deep sleep. They all kept rolling on their improvised beds, and every time they tried to close their eyes, their imaginations played with them. They knew there was always some truth in legends, but they also knew that the one they had gotten themselves involved with was not a traditional one. Fear monster's did not seem to have any invented part.

The next morning, they got up at around 9 a.m. They did not know how long their exploring would take and thus had agreed to not get started too late, just in case. Besides, they still had to go to Abby's and Gabe and Theresa's to pick up some lanterns, jackets and something to eat and drink.

When they went downstairs, they did not find it strange that Mary was not around when they went to pick up their stuff. After all, the elderlies had said that they were not able to say anything other than what they had already said, so they might have decided to not be around to avoid any temptation. Thus, when they were done filling their backpacks, they left to the forest without saying goodbye.

'How do you reckon we should name the forest?' said Theresa once they walked past the last house in the urban area.

'Why do we need a name for it anyway?' asked Mark. He had become less irritable, yet he still managed to demonstrate that he had not taken the leading attitude at any moment.

'Why not? I mean, we would still have to name it, so why not make up a name for it? Besides, that could have us entertained until we reach the border. I reckon we still have a good one hour walk,' replied Theresa, pointing with her hand towards the forest they were heading to.

'How about The Forest?' suggested Gabe. Seeing the reaction of his sister, he hurried to add: 'Oh, come on Theresa! Why is it so important for you that it has a name? It is just a bloody name. Anything would do'.

'Our grannies got really pissed off when I suggested Fear monster wasn't but a book character. And they made it very clear that we should not be impertinent. We shall take this seriously, you know' said Theresa, hurt. She could not understand why her brother was not seeing things as clearly as her. 'But let's ask someone with their brains on their place. What do you think, Nora?'.

The truth was, that she agreed with Theresa. She had realised that they should be behaving as grown-ups whenever they were doing anything that was related to the legend. Yet she did not know how to voice it so the boys would not get offended by their constant agreement on disagreeing with them.

'We know you agree with Theresa, Nora,' said Mark, taking her back from her daydreaming. 'So go ahead and tell us what's your name suggestion'.

She cursed herself for her unwanted ability to show her emotions on her face regardless of her willingness to do so, and said: 'The Enchanted Forest'.

'That's just the fangirls version of my proposal!' said Gabe, holding his laugh. 'You just made it fancier. Why would it be any more suitable?'.

They kept discussing the suitability of Nora's name suggestion for what was remaining of their way to the forest's border. It became a sort of boys versus girls type of discussion, where neither of them would give in to any of their counterpart's ideas. Albeit that, they did have a good time discussing their differences. That helped them to get to know each other a bit more before reaching the first trees. Once there, they sat in a circle and placed the book in the middle. The protagonists had said that they were going to be provided with a map, so they better have it before they got lost.

And like it had happened before, the book opened itself right where it needed to be opened: the second protagonists' letter. Again, they witnessed how the next blank page was magically doodled.

Dear dauntless readers,

Congratulations! You have reached the border of our domains.

We are happy that you have taken into consideration our warnings, and that you have not tried to discover anything beforehand. We much appreciate that, and thus we will provide you with a gift.

We are aware that you have prepared yourselves with lanterns and food, but fear not, we will not let anything happen to you (should you behave, of course). For that reason, please do take these necklaces with you. They are on us.

Before we sign out however, we would like to add something. Please, do forgive our meddling, but we do like Nora's name suggestion. Our vote goes to The Enchanted Forest. We believe that undoes the tie, and thus provides us with a name.

Yours sincerely,

The protagonists.

As soon as the letter was fully written, the page turned and four necklaces were quickly doodled onto the next blank page. They had been expecting that to happen, as they had been told that they were going to be gifted some. What took them all by surprise however was the fact that once the last detail of the last necklace to be drawn was finished, it caused a blinding light to be produced. It only lasted for a few seconds, but it was enough to make them lose sight of what was happening in front of them. When the brightness was decreased, they found out that the necklaces that had been drawn on their book were now lying on top of it.

Rubbing her eyes for them to stop tearing, Nora extended a hand to pick up one necklace, but she could not choose any. Instead, one of them chose her before she was able to grab any of them. Her hand was only a few inches away from the one that was closest to her, when the one that was furthest flew all over from the centre of the circle to her hand. Once she was able to hold it, she stared at it, astonished. It was a beautiful, golden coated sphere, with some inscriptions over the edge that she was not able to read at the time. To allow for comfortable handling, it was provided with an also golden coated thin strip.

'Listen!' exclaimed Theresa when she was about to put the necklace on. 'I've either gone nuts or that pendant is playing some music'.

Nora had been so absorbed by the sudden events, that Theresa shouting startled her so badly. Such was the case, that she let her go off her necklace. When she kneeled to grab it from the floor, she realised Theresa was indeed right. Her pendant was producing a very soft melody that was known to her. Yet again, she could not tell why it sounded so familiar. Regardless, should Theresa had not pointed it out, it would have passed completely unnoticed to the other three.

'I've got the feeling it's the same melody I heard when I first opened the book,' said Mark, breaking the silence they had imposed over themselves. 'Although... it didn't seem that repetitive last time. It is as though only the first cords were being played, over and over again. I still can't tell which is the song they belong to though. I'm pretty sure I have heard it before. Any wild guesses, piano wonder girl?' he added, rubbing his head while turning to look at Nora.

'Not a clue, no,' said Nora. She, like Mark, had felt that melody as a familiar one, although neither of them was able to tell when they had heard it before. She had only had two chances to listen to it when regarding the book, but the more she tried to think of which composition it was, the further away she felt from finding out which one it was.

'Leaving the melody aside, I think we should get going. I don't wanna be in here at night time,' said Gabe. The moment he finished talking, he tried to grab one of the necklaces, but the necklace that was meant for him jumped straight to his hand the moment he made the decision to take one.

As for Theresa and Mark, the same happened to them when they decided to take theirs. Thus, when the four of them had been provided with the necklaces, the book shut close and the melody that Nora's pendant was producing, stop playing altogether.

10

*D*ear mum,

How are things back in Scotland? How's dad doing? I hope he's seriously dealing with his flight fear so you can drop me a visit some time. I'd like to tour you around Hamburg.

University is going alright. Engineering is difficult enough on its own, let alone in German, but I'm coping. I've improved my language skills a lot, and Aksel is proved a very helpful colleague. I'm sure I have already told you how we met, but just in case I'll remind you of him.

When I first arrived here in Hamburg, I didn't know where to go or what to do, so I paid a lot of attention to details. By that time I was observing people a lot, just to figure out who I might want to become friends with. Aksel and I were taking pretty much the same courses, so it was just a matter of time that we started talking. In the beginning, I thought he was a senior at university, but it turned out that he was also an exchange student! Why did I get that impression then? Well, I guess it was because he was really popular. There was not a time that he walked on the aisles that he was not interjected by anyone. And he played cool. I guess he liked that, regardless of what he says now.

We were assigned to do a couple of peer workshops together, so our friendship grew a lot from midterm onwards. He invited me to cafés, to the movies,... he even set up library study dates for us. I felt comfortable with him, so I never said no. He was a really good teacher, but overall, he was a very good friend as well.

Any time I had a rough day, he would help me out. He wouldn't let me be sad for more than how much it took me to explain to him why I was feeling that way. He had (and still does) the capability of always ending up stealing a smile from me. I think that was the part that made me fall in love with him.

When I went home for Christmas, we had already started dating more seriously, but I didn't say anything because I didn't want to bring my expectations too high. I liked him from the very first time I saw him, but to be honest, I never thought he'd set eyes on me. He had a whole university behind him, why me then?

I know that you, being my mother, would think that any boy would love to be with me, but I don't see it that way. Anyway, this wasn't supposed to be a letter about me. Well yes. I mean, a letter about my life in Hamburg, not my love life.

Long story short, when I came back to Germany, Aksel wanted to go more serious about our relationship. He said that over Christmas he had realised that he wanted to spend his lifetime with me, so we made it official. And on the first midterm holidays, he invited me over to his parents' in Austria.

It was a beautiful time, mum. Such a lovely country! The scenery is gorgeous, and the

Austrians are really welcoming. We should visit some time together.

While we were in Austria, Aksel walked me around his hometown. He took me to his former school, as well as to the parks he used to play at, and his football club. I met a lot of people that he grew up with, but there was someone who stood over the rest.

Her name is Klara. She was Aksel's first primary school teacher. In the beginning, I was really surprised that she'd recognised Aksel; you know, it had been ages since he had left school. But it turns out she is friends with Aksel's parents. What really impressed me though, was the fact that she looks a lot like you. Her eyes are the same as yours, and so are her chin and her hair curls. What a coincidence, right?

I'm looking forward to your reply. I miss you lots.

Your Nora.

- X -

Once they were all equipped with their respective necklaces, Nora grabbed the book and put it back in her backpack. She then put her necklace around her neck and started walking. She was as clueless as her friends about where they should head to, yet they decided to follow the dirt road that run in between the trees, as it looked like the only way to go inside The Enchanted Forest.

They walked and walked inside the forest, with the dirt road itself as a guide, until they reached an intersection.

'I knew it couldn't be that easy!' exclaimed Mark. 'We've had a pleasant walk all the way up to here. Which direction do you reckon we should continue on?' he ended up asking, rubbing his head.

'Well, I guess we could just wait to be told which direction we shall take,' said Gabe, sitting on a rock by the edge of the dirt road. 'I mean, we were told we'd be helped, so I'll wait until that help arrives. Do you want some snacks?' he added, taking a small bag of crisps from his backpack.

'Oh Gabe, please! Haven't you learned anything so far?' asked Theresa, exasperated. 'We are not playing hide-and-seek here. We've been told that our lives wouldn't be at risk, but I wouldn't bet on that. It's true we have been helped somehow so far, but there wasn't a single time that we were told something that we hadn't guessed ourselves beforehand. We will only get our responses confirmed, but we have to play our cards to try and figure them out. You'll be left to die sitting on that rock unless you show some interest in the legend'.

'Faaar point well maaee, sis,' said Gabe while swallowing what was remaining of his crisps bag. Putting the rubbish into his backpack, he stood up and said: 'Then let's have a look at the book. Maybe a map was doodled on it'.

Nora heartfully doubted a map would have been doodled on the legends book. It was true that the book had proved to have an unlimited amount of resources, but she did not think a map would be it. Or at least not just then. They had been gifted four necklaces that had to be of some use on their journey.

From the moment they had started walking deeper into the forest, she had played with the strip around her fingers while staring at the sphere that hanged from it. It only had a few inches of diameter, so despite the clear fact that it had some scribbles on it, she had been completely unable to tell what they were. Yet she was so sure, that the answer to their direction-wise dilemma would be cleared out should they discover how to use the pendants in their favour.

'Why are you staring at me?' asked Nora when she realised the other three were following all her movements.

'You haven't listened to a word we've said, have you?' asked Theresa back.

'Other than your brother thinks a map was doodled on the book, you mean?'.

'You should be less obvious next time, Nora,' said Gabe. 'You might hurt someone's feelings someday'.

'What do you mean by that?' asked Nora, hurt by Gabe's comment. She was sure that she had been daydreaming and that it had all been projected on her face, but she had explained herself before for her strange capability. As much as Gabe did not want to understand that, she could not help it.

'What my brother wanted to say…,' said Theresa, looking daggers at her brother, 'is that we've been talking about which direction to take. We've got a 33% probability of getting it right, which isn't a lot, so we've agreed to not make a move until we feel we've made a decision based on rational thinking. For that reason, we've been asking you to hand us the book, so we could go back to what we have already. Just in case something has passed unnoticed'.

Ashamed for her daydreaming, Nora took the book from her backpack and handed it to Theresa. She did not think the answer would be on the book but in the necklaces. Yet she did not feel her word would count much on that precise moment. Not after she had been caught not listening to what they had been saying. For that reason, she left her three friends with the book and positioned herself right in the middle of the crossroad, leaving the dirt road they had followed up to there at her back.

She felt that, out of the three dirt roads that laid in front of her, just one would take them to the monster's dwelling, although she could not tell which one. They all looked the same to her from her position. Neither looked scarier nor safer. There were no marks, or signs, or footprints that would suggest choosing one over the others. Yet she remained in that position, thinking hard. If they had been brought to that site, it was because they needed to surpass that challenge.

Still standing in the same position, she closed her eyes and grabbed the pendant with her right hand. She remained like that for a couple of seconds only, but felt a beat coming from the sphere the moment her fingers completely embraced it.

'You know what, I'm pretty sure we're to get the answer through the necklaces,' she shouted, turning around to reunite with her friends. 'Forget about the book, at least for the time being'.

'Why? How?' asked Gabe. He was still feeling resentful, and he did not make any effort to hide that.

Pushing aside the anger that that tinge on Gabe's words had produced on her, Nora related what she had just experienced. It was very difficult to put it into words. But she was sure she had felt as though the pendant wanted to communicate with her, somehow. Thus, she urged them to imitate her, but none were able to experience the same as she had.

'Maybe it's because you're not in the right position. Try coming here,' she said while grabbing Theresa to take her to where she had stood. She then helped her to be oriented as she had been, and before stepping back, she whispered in her ear: 'Faith will help you'.

Theresa took a few deep breathes before closing her eyes. She then took a couple more with her eyes closed before tightening her fingers around the pendant. And like it had happened to Nora, the moment she completely embraced the sphere, she felt it beating.

'Nora's right!' she exclaimed. 'Gabe, Mark! Come here and do as she says! If you believe it will provide you with answers, then you'll feel it committing to you. Come!' she hurried them up.

A bit hesitant, the boys stood up and joined them in the middle of the intersection. They then placed themselves side by side facing the dirt road in the middle, closed their eyes and then embraced the pendant. Their reaction was as quick as the girls had been.

'And now what?' asked Gabe.

'You tell us,' said Nora. Realising that Gabe had not understood her double sense, she added: 'Your sphere, Gabe. It's leading the way'.

Gabe looked down at his chest and found out that his sphere was glowing and moving towards the path on the right.

11

While wiping the tears that were flooding her eyes, Eileen folded the letter and gave it back to her grandmother. She just could not believe everything that she had been told. It all seemed to be very unrealistic. Yet she had been shown proofs that confirmed her grandmother's relating. Her mother had indeed met someone in a German-speaking country named Klara. And as difficult as it was to believe, that person had undoubtedly written both the letter that had been hidden on the back of the frame that had hanged on her room for fifteen years and the contract that Leagsaidh had signed when she was in her late teenage years. And maybe it was that certainty that did not make it any less painful.

All of a sudden, her whole family tree had been changed. She was aware of the early passing of Bhaltair, but there was another branch to be added at the same level, that whoever knew whether or not it was the node to a different extension of the crown. As for her grandfather, she could not start understanding everything that might have gone through his brains…

Very smoothly, Alick stood up from the armchair he had been sitting on, and extended his hand to his wife, for her to hand him Nora's letter. He quickly read it, without an obvious change on his grimace.

'I recall reading this letter when it arrived,' he said, giving the letter back to his wife. 'Why did ye never mention that that Klara was yer sister?'.

'Well, I wasn't sure at the moment,' said Leagsaidh, trying to sound convincing. 'I can't deny I suspected she'd be, but I had to make sure befo'e opening that door. It's not pleasant to talk 'bout how one once got their heart torn into pieces'.

'So I guess that's why ye arranged fer Aksel's parents to go to Hamburg to meet up with us, instead of us visiting them in Austria. Is that correct?'.

The change on Leagsaidh's grimace was the answer that Alick had been looking for. He was not feeling angry towards her whatsoever, yet he needed something that would alleviate the burden that the latest events had put on his shoulders. In the beginning, he had felt insulted, but what his wife had shared right afterwards had proved to him that her intentions had always been noble. She had tried to protect them all, although whether he approved of her ways, that was something to be discussed some other time.

He still had many questions to ask her, although he did not know how much deeper he could dig without his wife breaking apart. He wanted her to feel he was there for her no matter what, not quite the opposite, so he decided that he would continue with his questioning in the morning. Thus, he stood up and walked towards her to kiss her goodnight, but just when he was about to kiss her forehead, Leagsaidh started talking again:

'I haven't seen Clarissa since she left the village. We know she was alive 25 years ago, but I can't tell whether she still is. Besides, I don't know whether I'm ready to face her, should she still be around. But please, don't force me to do anything. Healing processes are different frem person to person'.

The ability that Leagsaidh had to answer unasked questions was something that had amazed Eileen for her entire life. It was true that she herself had inherited from her the ability to observe and go beyond words, but she had never been able to go to that extent.

Shaking her head for her to think clearly again, she deemed it convenient to help her grandparents to get ready for bedtime. It had been long since Alick and Leagsaidh had changed their bedroom to the room downstairs, so once they had settled, she headed to the stairs by herself. She was not feeling tired whatsoever, but she considered going to her room to put her thoughts in order was her best chance.

When she re-entered the room, she saw the glass fragments that were still laying on the floor. She had experienced so much since she had left the room in the morning, that she had not had a single moment to think of what she had left behind. As for the broken, disassembled frame, it was on her desk, together with the thumbtacks, right next to her laptop.

She had promised herself that that summer she would fight for what she had always dreamed about: writing a full-length novel. She still had the idea in her head, although it was fading away the more she worked on her former Nora story. Although just a few pages long, and written a long time ago, it had never left her. She had indeed named the protagonist after her mother. They had only shared her first year together before her parents had died in a car crash, so she had thought that something of hers being in the centre of one of her creations was the least she could do to honour her memory.

She had in her head other adventures for the young red-haired Nora, but she was still maturing her first one. It was indeed taking much longer than she had thought, yet she was enjoying the process. It had turned out to be very useful to keep her mind away from the fact that she had planned to be done over her holidays. She was only just then starting to realise that she had been way too optimistic. She might one day be done with her novel, but not with her current circumstances.

Both Klara's and her mother's letters kept coming back to her head. Her grandmother had said that the fact they had both met could not be called but destiny, and as much as she despised the idea of believing in fate, she could not find any other explanation. Miles and miles had separated them for years, yet the family had managed to reunite somehow. Out of all the guys her mother could have dated while studying abroad, she had ended up hanging out with an Austrian guy that had been taught by her great aunt.

'*How crazy!*' thought Eileen while switching on her computer.

She still had contact with her grandfather on her dad's side of the family, although she did not have a chance to ask him. He had been diagnosed with Alzheimer a few months before. He was being taken care of at a nursing home, but he was quickly losing his memory. The last time they had face-timed through one of the nurses' phone, he had been completely unable to recognise her, let alone remember someone he might have not seen since they moved to southern Germany after her father had graduated from university.

She considered the possibility of going on social media to try and find something from her great aunt, but she did not know where to start from. All she knew was her maiden name, and that was not enough. Given that she had refused to use her English name, she would have undoubtfully taken Leon's surname. And unfortunately for her, she had no idea what his family name was.

Once the screen of her laptop went live, she pushed aside with all her will all the thoughts about her newly discovered relatives and opened her *Novel in progress* file. She truly felt the need to go back to her pulling the strings. She needed time with herself She could go back to the attic the next morning.

- XI -

They had been told that they would be provided with a way of getting straight to the cave once they were in the forest. A map had been mentioned in the protagonists' last letter, although they might have not meant it in a literal way. It was magic they were dealing with, so maybe they were making sure that only the people meant to find their cave got provided with the directions towards it.

Making sure they were not leaving anything behind them, they renewed their journey towards the monster's dwelling. Gabe positioned himself at the front of the retinue, for his sphere to lead their way.

'Nora…?' he asked just a few minutes after they had started walking again. Nora jogged to catch up with him and nodded her head for him to continue talking. 'I'm sorry for having been rude before. I reckon you were thinking of what our chances were, so I shouldn't have talked to you that way. Will you accept my apologies?'.

'Indeed I will, Gabe,' she said, grabbing his hand to reassure him on her saying. 'The situation is complicated enough for us to fight. Besides, I should have told you what I was thinking of. We could have all worked it out together faster. Four heads might have found a solution first'.

'I doubt there is a head any clever than yours, to be honest,' he said, returning the reassuring hand grab. 'Why do you think mine reacted differently, though? I mean, you were the one who discovered how to use the pendants. Why didn't yours lead the way?'.

Gabe had so many doubts as to why his was telling them where to go. If it had not been for his sister and Nora, he would have remained sitting on that rock for as long as he had

had snacks to keep him entertained. He had not given a thought a bit further, as they have done. Then why on earth was his sphere glowing and shifting directions as though it were a compass?

Nora was asking herself the same questions. She had always taken the leading attitude, although Theresa had worked things out a good amount of times. Yet the four of them made a whole. Should just one of them be left behind, they would be missing a piece. They were not able to mount the puzzle just then, but she was sure that all of them were to play an important part. After all, her grandmother had said *'I'm afraid that given the circumstances, you can't be left aside'*. And she was feeling confident that she had not made that comment unintentionally.

Without letting go of Gabe's hand, they kept walking deeper into the forest. It was not until Mark started complaining about feeling hungry, that they took a break and stopped for lunch. They found a grass patch in between the trees, sat in a circle, and started swallowing their sandwiches.

'I've been thinking of why Gabe's pendant has reacted beyond ours, but I can't come with an idea. Any guesses?' asked Nora once she was done with her sandwich. She had not realised how hungry she was until she had started eating.

'May I correct you...? You've been thinking of Gabe. Full stop,' said Mark with a mischievous look on his face. 'Wow, wow. Stop with the pebble throwing! I haven't spoken but the truth!' he quickly added when he was found the target of his friends' projectiles.

Nora noticed her freckled face reddening, so she started moving faster for her to disguise it as her becoming hot due to physical exercise. While doing that, she hoped that her willingness to not be caught red-handed really worked that time. Yet regardless of what they had thought, that relaxed moment full of laughs did help to take the tension out of their heads. At least for a couple of minutes.

'Recentring on our business,' said Theresa, glancing at Mark for him to stop giggling, 'I have also been thinking about why my brother's pendant reacted differently. While I re-read what we have so far, I didn't come across anything that stood out whatsoever; I had everything in my head already. But that doesn't precisely mean that I was looking at it from the right angle. One can't see but what they want to see'.

'Could you be any more specific, please?' said Mark, quitting his giggling all at once.

'Haven't you realised it too, Nora?' asked Theresa, pretending not to have listened to what Mark had just said. For the first time since they had started their adventure, Nora did not have a clue about what Theresa was saying, so when she shook her head no, she resumed: 'And what if I say the scrawls aren't meaningless? Does that give you any clue?'.

Nora and the boys were not expecting Theresa to throw another question at them, so when she decided to keep on enquiring them, they felt insulted. She had literally been asked to say what she thought once and for all, and instead, she had decided to keep on with the interrogation! The boys voiced their concerns about it very clearly, whilst Nora started her daydreaming.

Theresa had said that the scrawls they had gotten when they had first opened the books were not meaningless. Each of them had gotten a different one, and now that she came to think about it, the protagonists had never done anything accidentally. There had always been a purpose behind their acts.

The fact that their four books had collapsed into one, together with the warning that her grandmother had made, that was becoming clearer as they kept on unravelling things, suggested that the four of them made the whole. They all for sure had their weak and strong points, and they were to support on each other's strengths to surpass the challenges that they were to find on their way. A single piece going missing would leave the puzzle unfinished for eternity.

Yet everything had started as a one person's business.

Each of them had experienced the urge to be by themselves when they were to open the book for the first time. They had been warned about what the future may hold for them, and they had been given the clues to succeeding in their endeavours. To start with, they had been shown that magic was a thing in their world. They needed believing before being shown anything else, and they had needed to achieve that individually. Thus, by fulfilling that task, they had earned the right to face the next challenge, which Nora was coming to realise that had been the fact that they were to work as a single, yet multi-assembled piece.

Everything had happened so fast that she had not had time to think about it, but now that she had been guided on to what to think, she did not have doubts anymore. The book had recognised them before they were able to recognise themselves. Each one of them had been assigned a task that was to be fulfilled for them to get to the end of it all.

'You're a genius, Theresa!' exclaimed Nora, feeling really confident about her thoughts.

'Oh, please, I'm not. I haven't done much, have I?' she asked with a gleeful shine on her eyes. Her feminine instinct was telling her that Nora had reached the same conclusion as she had.

'I don't think you have, sis,' said Gabe. Turning towards Nora, he added: 'could you please explain yourself? This dude and I have missed something,', he said, pointing at Mark.

'You're just not seeing it from the right angle. That's all' said Nora. Realising that the boys were about to complain, she silenced them with a flip of her hand, and continued talking: 'have a look at your pendants. What would you expect to be scrawled on them?'.

Both Gabe and Mark did as they were told, and when they realised what the girls had been trying to say, they could not help excitement from overflooding their limbic systems. They had again succeeded in unravelling a critical step on their journey to discovering the truth about Fear monster's legend.

'Gabe will guide us through the forest, whilst I will be able to track Fear monster's trail. Mark will be able to tell which one is the actual dwelling, should there be more than just one cave. And you, Nora, you will discover what the melody did, or does, or will do' said a joyful Theresa.

12

Eileen worked on her novel until dawn. Due to her long sleep the evening before, she was able to work for about three hours without stopping. The house had been quiet and the soft music she had played to concentrate had done its job so well, that she had a bunch of new chapters to send to her grandfather. Thus, she considered emailing him her progress and then going to bed. A couple of hours of deep sleep before lunchtime would be enough for her to get through the day.

She woke up a few hours later when her alarm went off. She did not feel at all like getting out of bed, but she considered that was the best option she had. Otherwise, it will take her days to go back to a normal eating-sleeping schedule. Hence, she jumped out of bed, put on some clean clothes and went downstairs for lunch.

She joined her grandparents for lunch in the dining room. It took her a while though to realise that albeit what had happened the night before, her grandparents were treating each other as though their conversation about Klara had not existed at all. They were as kind to each other as she has always seen them being.

'You'll have to tell me your secret one day,' she said, sitting at the dining table.

'What do ye mean?' asked Alick, taken aback. He clearly was not getting where his grandchild was going.

'The ability you guys have to get over anything that disturbs your lives,' she said. 'I mean, after what grandma told us last night, I wouldn't blame you for being angry at her for weeks! But the next morning, you guys are...like you've always been!' she exclaimed, excited. She was not telling her grandparents off whatsoever, she was just amazed by how quickly they had gone back to normal.

'Ye know what, deary,' said Alick, pouring himself some vegetable soup on his dish, 'my dad used to tell me: if ye've got a problem, and it does have a solution, then ye don't have a problem anymore. Likewise, if ye've got a problem, and it does not have a solution, then ye don't have a problem anymore either.

»Yer happiness should only depend on ye. It's a status that ye have to acquire from within ye. And it may sometimes require forgiveness, whether frem ye or towards ye, and a bunch of other times it might just be enough through coldness. Whichever ye're on however, do rely on what yer heart tells ye to do' he added while softly kissing his wife's hand.

'I will indeed, grandpa,' said Eileen. Why her grandfather was feeling so philosophical, she had no idea, but she decided to leverage the situation and try to go back to the topic that they had discussed the night before. 'When I went to my room last night, I considered going to the attic to go through my parents' stuff. But then I thought it would have been rude of me to do it without letting you know in advance. I know grandma can't really join me up there, so I was thinking that I could bring everything down here, and the three of us could do the research. I'm sure something passed unnoticed last time. Now that we know a bit more about my mum's whereabouts, we could find something that we'll lead us to discover whether or not Klara, or Clarissa, however we decide to name her, is still alive'.

'I'd stick to Clarissa,' said Leagsaidh. She sounded a bit uncomfortable, yet she agreed to Eileen's suggestion: 'Please, do take all those boxes to the living room. I might be able to find a solution to an all-time problem of mine'.

Eileen did not need anything else to make her day that day. It filled her heart to know that her grandmother was willing to go through her parents' stuff once again. Ever since she had been unravelled her own story, she had been allowed to go to the attic whenever she had wanted to. In the beginning, she had spent endless hours up there, just by herself, but as she had grown up, she had started spending less and less time surrounded by the boxes that contained the things that had once belonged to her parents. She had never forgotten about them though, it was just that she had found a different way to deal with the fact that she had been left parentless from such a young age.

She had however taken with her the things that she had liked the most, like that one green scarf that had once belonged to Aksel. She had carried that one with her for years. Thus, when she was done with her lunch, she hurried upstairs and brought with her all the boxes that were labelled as 'Nora & Aksel'.

Her grandparents had kept a lot of her parents things, yet once she was told all about them, the three of them had agreed to throw away whatever was no longer of any use. They had mostly gotten rid of old clothes and old-fashioned gadgets. They had kept all the letters, as well as Nora's university notes, so Eileen was feeling confident that they would be able to find something that would lead them straight to Clarissa.

As soon as Eileen brought down the last of the boxes, the three of them started going through everything that was inside of them. In the past, they had classified everything according to whether they were personal or non-personal things. For instance, all the letters that Aksel had once written to Nora were in the same box, which was the one that Nora chose to go through first.

She had endless times fallen asleep reading her dad's love letters to her mum back when they were dating. Because they had been an international couple, they had not found it disturbing to sometimes write in English, sometimes in German, and sometimes even in both at a time. In the beginning, she had found that quite challenging, but once she was gifted a German dictionary for her tenth birthday, she quit imagining what his dad had said. She had never taken German lessons, yet she had managed to learn the basics with the help of her Austrian grandparents.

Eileen reread every single letter that was in the box. She got very emotional over some of them, yet because she was so determined to find out something about her great aunt, she did not succumb to tears. It was not until the last letter she read, that she could find a reference to Clarissa. It was one of the last letters that Aksel had written to Nora during the year before she moved to Germany:

Liebe Nora,

Ich freue mich, dass alles mit der Universität gut läuft. Das ist das gleiche für mich. Ich arbeite bereits an meiner Abschlussarbeit. Ich mag das Thema, obwohl es überhaupt nicht einfach ist. Nichtsdestotrotz arbeite ich hart daran, dass ich dich in Schottland besuchen kann.

I'm dying to meet your parents. It was very kind of them writing me that letter you sent me last time. Auch wird es mein erstes Mal in Großbritannien sein. I know it's months apart yet, but I can't wait to see Highland cows. They're so exotic to me!

Anyway, Klara (a friend of my parents' and my first primary school teacher, do you remember her?) was around last week. We were talking about everything and nothing, and when I mentioned that I was going to visit you in the summer, she told me that she's never told us, but that she had been born in northern Scotland. Verrückt, oder? She also said that she moved to Germany with her husband when she was very young, so because her kids had been born in Germany, she felt German herself. She speaks English perfectly of course, but she doesn't sound like you whatsoever. She's lost the accent, somehow.

Themen ändern sich, ich bekam eine Benachrichtigung von der Stelle, für die ich mich beworben hatte. Und Überraschung...I got the place! As soon as I graduate university, I'll go back to Hamburg for work. It's a very big enterprise; it might receive thousands of applications, and I managed to get one! It's nuts. Vielen Dank für die Ermutigung mich zu bewerben. You give me the confidence I lack sometimes. I can't wait for us to live again in the country that brought us together.

Send greetings to your parents on my behalf.

Ich liebe dich,

Deine Aksel.

- XII -

The moment she had placed the necklace around her neck and stared at the sphere, Nora had noticed that there was something scribbled on the edges. Back then however, she had not been able to tell what that was. But since she had been guided towards the truth of the story, a shift had been made in the way she approached the existence of the pendants.

Although if it had not been for Theresa, she would have never thought about the scrawls not being meaningless. She had wondered why each of them had gotten a different thing, yet because they all seemed to have a connexion with the legend, she had not given any more thoughts to it. Yet, the more she thought about the conclusion they had just reached, the more she realised that it had been there all the time for them.

Mark had gotten a cave because it represented the monster's dwelling, and it could not have been coincidental. Out of the four of them, he had been the one who had felt the most reluctant to do the exploring. As though the protagonists had known it beforehand, they had tagged him with the representation of a limited enclosure, which so perfectly mimicked his not-out-of-my-comfort-zone behaviour. He was a cool and chill guy, who made tons of jokes when he was feeling safe, but that turned into a very annoying dude when he was forced to go against his will.

As for Gabe, he had been tagged with a forest. It also represented a limited enclosure, but that nonetheless was wider and more liable to guidance. Forests are not just made up of trees but of many different living forms. They are big ecosystems made of millions of smaller ecosystems, that form a whole through their interactions. *'Alike him, forests are strong by themselves, yet vulnerable to strangers'* thought

Nora, laughing to her insides. She had caught herself clumsily smiling whenever she thought of Gabe, and that made her feel in a way she had not felt ever before. It was a feeling she did not know how to deal with, and the fact that everything that she was feeling got reflected on her face, made her quickly start thinking of the connection of Theresa with her scrawl:

'Out of the four of us, she is the most proof-driven. She observes everything and does not make a decision until she is one hundred per cent sure. She trusts her guts, yet she analyses everything thoroughly. She is capable of changing her perspective for the good, despite that meaning she has to throw away her previous theory. And, on top of that, she is also capable of making others realise the truth through their own means. She truly does set up a path that is easy to follow for others'.

Nora was able to link the scrawls her friends had gotten with the personality she knew of them. The moment she had realised what Theresa was so cryptically meaning, all those ideas had come to her head. It had been as though she had been standing in a dark room, and someone had suddenly switched on the lights: the facts had always been there, although she had not been able to see them as they were. As for herself however, she was having more trouble finding the connection.

She was sure that the fact she was a pianist had not passed unnoticed to the protagonists, however that information had been known to them. Yet she had the feeling there was more to it. Thus, having learned her lesson before, she decided to share her thoughts with her friends. She told them how she thought they were linked to their scrawls, putting all her efforts into trying to stop her from blushing when she talked about Gabe.

'Yet I'm not sure about how I fit into the story,' she said, feeling a little bit uncomfortable. She did not like exposing her emotions in public. 'I reckon me being a pianist undoubtedly links me to musical notes, but there must be more to it. So… I guess I could use some help now,' she added, looking at the three of them, pleading assistance.

'I've told you before, Nora,' said Gabe, standing up and offering his hand to her. 'There is no head cleverer than yours in here right now. You are capable of creating abstract art through a different coding system. It takes time and dedication to become what you are, as well as an innate ability'.

'My brother is right, I guess,' said Theresa, all of a sudden. She had noticed the hidden meaning of what her brother had just said, yet she evaded stepping on that land. 'I mean, scores aren't but a different way of scripting. They are made of different symbols and are much more complex than one expects at the beginning. Regardless, they lead to the creation of art, whatever one understands by art. You musicians can mentally transport people to different places with your creations. You can even bring back memories and sensations!' she enthusiastically exclaimed. Realising that her friends had still not reached her conclusion, she resumed: 'What I'm trying to say is that you can *lead* what people think'.

'Oh…oh…,' was all Nora could say. Theresa's intervention had genuinely left her speechless.

From a very young age, she had had to deal with the fact that people praised her. It had never gotten to her head, yet even though she had gotten used to that, any time that people had gone a bit more personal about their praising, she had gotten uncomfortable. She just did not know what to say back other than '*Ooh.. thank you. Yet anyone can do that actually*' or '*That's very kind of you. Thank you*'.

'Even though your hypothesis leaves me as no less than an outsider,' said Mark, bringing them all back from their daydreaming, 'I can't deny you've got your point. Although, how do they know I'd behave like that? I mean, the scrawls were there even before we met Nora. How did the protagonists know she'll be our *leader*?' he said, emphasizing the word leader, 'or that Theresa would work everything out?'.

'That's a very good question, indeed,' said Theresa. She enjoyed quizzical challenges, and by the joy in her face, it seemed she was accepting that one. 'I'm assuming that our grannies have had something to do. You know, they listened to my relating as though we were talking about the weather broadcast. And they were pretty mystical about it all. It was as though they wanted to help us but feared saying too much'.

'So?' asked Mark again. Alike the protagonists had so well predicted, he did not like stepping out of his comfort zone.

'I don't know just yet, Mark. I'll have to give it a thorough thought,' said Theresa, putting on a face. She had started wondering that the moment Nora had told them about her hypothesis. Even though she had not voiced her thoughts, she had followed the same way of thinking. She had no doubts that she would have reached the same point, regardless of how much time it would have taken her.

Having unravelled yet another mystery, they continued walking into the forest, unaware that the closer they were getting to Fear monster's dwelling, the more they were being watched.

13

Eileen was aware that the fact that Clarissa was mentioned in one of the letters, did not help them much just then. Yet having found her name made her feel confident. It proved that her parents had indeed left written references to that mysterious woman, so there was a chance that, with patience, they would be able to find a way to contact her.

Tidying everything around her, she raised her head and said: 'I've got something'.

She handed the letter to her grandparents, whose faces had acquired a worried look. She realised that, deep down, their willingness to collaborate in the research had been motivated by the fact that, should they be able to find anything, they would not be able to link it with Clarissa. Not after all those years.

'He was always a v'ry clever boy,' said Alick. 'He used to switch languages with such ease, that I think he was able to have different conversations at a time with yer mum and us. Oh, don' look at me like that, Eileen,' he added when he noticed that Eileen had gotten surprised by his latest comment, 'he was always v'ry polite. But he was also a German native. As good as his English was, he felt more comfortable speaking German. And I don' blame him, but I only understand half of this letter,' he added, handing the letter back to Eileen.

The moment she had given the letter to her grandparents, Eileen had known that they would only be able to read the bits that had been written in English. Thus, taking the letter back from her grandfather, she translated the German paragraphs:

'Dear Nora, I'm happy that everything is going well with university. It's the same for me. I'm already working on my thesis. I like the subject, although it is not easy at all. Nevertheless, I'm working hard to be able to visit you in Scotland. Blablabla,' she said, pointing the English words with her finger. When she reached a new German sentence again, she continued talking: 'it will be my first time in Great Britain.

»He then mentions the story of Klara, and when he says Verrückt, oder?, he means crazy, right? And then he completely changes topics and says that he had gotten a place at a very big enterprise in Hamburg, for which my mum had encouraged him to apply. He then says he loved her and signs it as Your Aksel'.

When she finished translating the letter to her grandparents, she did not know what else to do. She had gone through all the letters that her father had once written to her mother, yet she had only been able to find a very slight reference to the mysterious Klara. And it did not provide them with anything that they had not known. As for her grandparents, they had either not finished going through their boxes, or they had omitted something. To quit with the assumptions making, she decided to ask them: 'Have you found anything?'.

'Not yet,' said Alick. 'I've got the speed of an elder man, Eileen. Shall ye help me, we would be done quicker' he offered, lifting a few of the things that he had just taken from the box he had been searching into.

The box that Alick had been searching was full of Nora's university notes. It had hundreds of papers packed in different lots. They were mainly filled with calculations and diagrams, but should any reference had been made on any of them, it would have been almost impossible to spot unless she gave a thorough look to every single page. She considered the possibility but decided to aim for a quick glance first. If she succeeded, she would have saved so much time. And if she did not, well, she had already contemplated that possibility.

Eileen thus sat by her grandfather and took a thick paper lot that she put on top of her crossed legs. And when she did so, she laughed to her insides. Without having tried to find any lot in particular, she had managed to grab hold of the notes from the advanced physics course that her mother had taken when in Germany. She wished that luck visited her again and provided some light to their issue.

All the notes were of course written in German, although every now and then, a different hand lettering appeared to translate certain terms into English. The more she advanced on the lot, the more frequent those meddling scribbles became. In the beginning, she thought of the possibility of them being from her mum, as she herself had a completely different hand lettering when taking notes during a lecture than when she did not need to write that fast. But she discarded that possibility on the tenth page.

Because it was a physics course, it contained more calculations than actual text, which made it difficult to relate the hand lettering to anyone. Nonetheless, Eileen was able to figure it out. She remembered reading on the letter that her grandmother had handed her, that Nora had been on study dates with Aksel before they had adopted the girlfriend and boyfriend status. So it did not surprise her when she found a small drawing that intertwined an N and an A.

It did not surprise her, but it did make her feel emotional. A small tear dropped from her right eye when she blinked while passing her pointing finger over the drawing. She did not remember anything from the year she had shared with her parents, yet everything she had discovered about them made her feel as though she would have loved life with them. And it was not because she had not enjoyed herself with her grandparents, but because she found it very touching the way her father had been able to impress the love he felt towards Nora in every single letter he wrote her. As for her mother, she had never been able to read the letters she had once written to her German boyfriend because her Austrian grandparents, unlike her Scottish ones, had dwelled with the loss of Nora and Aksel in a different way.

The first time she had visited her grandparents in Germany she was ten years old. She had already been told who her parents were, and because she had been allowed to go to the attic to discover who they had been before her, she had dreamed of having an equally big reservoir at her other grandparents'. Unfortunately for her, almost everything that had once belonged to them, had been donated.

'*I'm sure you were as romantic, mum,*' thought Eileen. She was trying so hard to not collapse every time something touched her, that she could not help it when Alick said: 'I think I've got it'.

'What have you got, grandpa?' asked Eileen, leaving the papers she had been searching on lying open on the intertwined letters drawing.

'I might as well be wrong…,' he started saying. And even though Eileen took the paper he had just found from his hand, he resumed for Leagsaidh: 'but I think we've got a name. Her full name, I mean'.

And they did indeed. Eileen was founding it very difficult to hold her emotions. The moment she had heard from her grandfather that he might have been able to find something, she had started shaking and breathing heavily, but it was nothing compared to when she grabbed the paper herself and read what her mother had written so many years before:

Klara Herrmann. Dinner at 5 pm.

- XIII -

Nora, Theresa, Gabe and Mark continued walking deeper into the forest amongst laughs. They were for sure scared because of what they might encounter when they reached their destination. But it was precisely because of that that they were laughing. Although it was true that the feeling was completely different to when they had laughed at the park.

A worried tinge was tangible on their laughs, but one had to know them really well as to figure that out. To passers-by, they would have just looked like a friends gang that was having a good time together. The difference was however that no passers-by were wandering around the forest. The only eyes that were following them, were the eyes of the people they were unknowingly searching.

'What's wrong with you?' asked Mark. He had just collapsed into Theresa, who had suddenly stopped in the middle of the path, with her arms extended.

'Look,' was all Theresa said as a reply, pointing her right arm to the ground.

Because Nora had slightly fallen behind, she was able to not run into neither Theresa nor Mark. Mark's angry question had alerted her however, although it was nothing compared to when they saw what Theresa was pointing at. They all alternately looked from one to another, and the fact that Theresa's pendant started glowing only answered their unasked questions.

What lay right in front of them was, without any doubt, a Fear monster's footprint. It was a vast, human-like footprint, that nonetheless had some features that suggested that the foot that had impressed it onto the soil had some appendixes on the heel.

'What the…?' tried to exclaim Gabe, but because his sister turned around, he decided it was probably best to not end the sentence.

'Please, Gabe,' said Theresa, nodding her head no.

For the first time since she had met them, Nora saw a worried look on Theresa's face that made her shake. Something was telling her that her moment was getting closer faster than she expected, and she was afraid she might not be up to scratch. The look of the footprint itself was scaring enough on its own, together with the fact that, if they forced a look further away, they could discern a series of footprints that got lost on the very same horizon.

'It looks as they had just magically appeared,' said Mark when he recomposed.

'I…I…,' tried to say Theresa. Her feelings were tricking her, so she decided to take a couple of deep breaths before resuming: 'I've had the feeling for the last ten minutes or so, that we were being watched, somehow. I haven't said anything because I didn't want to scare you off, but we are not alone in here. Not that I thought we'd be, or that they wouldn't be expecting us. At the end of the day, we were directed here by the protagonists… But because I had been paying a lot of attention to details, I thought I'd be able to predict when my turn would arrive beforehand. It turns out I was wrong all along'.

Nora took pity on her. She stepped closer to her, tenderly caressed her on her arm, and wished for that gesture to be as comforting as she intended it to be. Given the circumstances, she did not think words would do any better than physical appreciation. Gabe positioned himself on the other side of Theresa and mimicked Nora.

After a few seconds, Mark decided to break the silence again: 'Guys, I want to be home by dinner time. As scary as it is, could we get going?'.

'As much as I despise the idea of moving without a plan, I assume from now on this is how it will be,' said Theresa, looking from her brother to Nora, and offering her hands for them to hold them.

'We could try and figure it out while we walk, can't we?' said Gabe, smiling at his sister and holding her hand tightly. Theresa responded to that stimuli by smiling back at her brother and softly squeezing his hand. After that, they both looked at Nora.

'I guess we could, yes,' she replied while also taking Theresa's hand on her own.

She had tried to impress to her voice all the courage she was able to find within her, but Nora was not sure she had accomplished her goal. Out of the four of them, she had been the one who had tried the hardest to convince the others it was their fate to do the exploring. She had felt excited, yet scared, at the very beginning and because the extraordinary events had been anything but useful since they had entered the boundaries of the forest, she had almost forgotten about the fact they were dealing with magic. But the sudden appearance of the footprints had completely twisted her heart.

Two of the pendants had already proven useful, which meant either Mark's or hers were the next ones to come into action. And she could not stop thinking about what her odds were. She was wishing for her to be the next one, as that way everything would not depend on her. But she was not feeling confident about that. The protagonists had recognised her as the leader of the group, however they had made that decision. So, as much as she did not want to think about it that way, she was starting to realise that she would be like the good skippers: the last to leave the ship.

Determined however to not succumb to her daydreaming yet again, she put all her efforts into bringing her concentration back into the conversation her friends were having. They were discussing how the footprints could have possibly appeared:

'I can't explain it, Mark,' was saying Theresa. She did not sound frustrated or annoyed, despite Mark having asked the same question a few times already. 'I've just got the feeling we're being watched. Neither do I know since when, nor whether it took a while for me to realise we were being watched, but I just feel eyes are observing us,' she added, moving her hands, which still were holding those of Gabe and Nora.

'I don't like that,' said Mark, turning around. Because he was the only one who was not holding hands with anyone, he had decided to take the lead and follow the footprints.

'I don't think our likes matter at all,' said Gabe, releasing his hand from his sister's. 'We are at a disadvantage here, but we have been the whole time. They knew our names even before we had *met* them' he said, emphasizing the word met.

'To be honest... It's been more of a monologue from them,' said Mark back. Nora was not sure whether he had intentionally wanted to sound annoyed, but he had indeed. 'I mean, we've gotten the letters for sure, and they've kept their word, but I don't think we've had any chance to chat back...'.

'And what would have you said? I don't think that would have provided us with any more details that we have now,' said Gabe. Like his sister, he did not sound annoyed when replying back to Mark.

'I would have asked them *why me?*' said Mark, as though that had been the most obvious question.

'Given that we are heading towards a meeting with that people, you could still ask them that,' said Gabe. 'Besides, should you have wasted your question in asking that, what benefit do you think you would have gotten?'.

'I could have made my decision based on something other than all my friends are going, for instance. And don't take me wrong, I'm not blaming you,' he quickly added when he realised his reply had irritated Gabe. 'I know I wasn't forced into this and, as Nora's grandma said, I hadn't really had a chance to decide…'.

'Technically you did,' said Nora. To her own surprise, she also sounded completely unannoyed, which cheered her up. 'Our names weren't scribbled into the books until we had agreed to read the legend. Not that I had wanted you to, but you could have left then'.

Mark opened his mouth to reply, but rethought what he had been about to say, and decided it was not appropriate for the moment. Instead, he turned around and decided to quit walking backwards. Yet he did not have much time to reconsider anything, because as suddenly as the footprints had appeared on their way, they disappeared. And we all know that he was not one that felt confident stepping outside of his comfort zone.

14

I t was, without any doubt, the neat handwriting of her mother. Every single *a* letter looked like the ones that had been once scribbled into the letter that Nora had sent to her parents whilst her exchange year abroad. And to Eileen, it was funny. Her own *a* letters looked like her mother's, even if she had acquired that habit long before she ever saw any of the papers that had been stored in the attic.

Trying to keep her feet on the ground however, Eileen closed her eyes and started thinking. It was true that they had found two references to someone named Klara so far, yet they could only be one hundred per cent sure one was of the person they had been searching for. Klara Herrmann could have been a very common name in German-speaking countries. Thus, as much as she wanted to remain sensible, she could not stop hope from being lit inside her. Her summer had been put upside down since she had found the letter hidden inside the frame. She had first planned for her to write a novel based on an idea she started having when she moved to Dundee, but she had not even started yet. Instead, days had passed whilst she had been rewriting her former red-haired Nora story. '*It turns out nothing will go as planned,*' she ended up saying to herself before opening her eyes again.

When she reopened her eyes, she found her grandparents were staring at her. They were both sitting still, although Alick was now sitting right beside his wife. While she had been focused on her thinking, he had taken one of the chairs from the dining table and had placed it right by Leagsaidh. When he saw Eileen was done with her inner battle, he said:

'It could have been a mate frem yer mum, Eileen. We need to remain sensible'.

'That… I know, grandpa. I am trying really hard to keep my hopes at bay. Yet you must agree with me, that we now have to keep searching. Maybe they wrote something else on their university notes, or…'.

'Or they hid another lette' inside a frame,' interrupted Leagsaidh.

'Do you really think so, grandma?' asked Eileen, taken aback. She was going to suggest that she could go check on social media while they kept on going through the boxes. But given that she only had a name, she could not apply any filters, so it was likely she would end up finding out nothing.

'We have neve' dismounted the frames, and it was where it all sta'ted,' said a calm Leagsaidh. Pointing at the box that contained Nora's university stuff, she added: 'we have the same chances as finding something scribbled on the university notes'.

'I think yer grandma is right, Eileen,' said Alick, taking his wife's hand to his mouth and kissing it softly. 'Nora hid a letter once. She could have hidden more'.

That idea had not come to Eileen at all before her grandmother had mentioned it, but she had to agree with them. Her mother had indeed once hidden a letter from her parents, so chances were she had done it yet another time. She could not understand why she had done that, but that was something she would have to deal with in a different moment, if at all. Unluckily for her, Nora was not there with them to answer all the questions she had, so unlike her mother had left it written somewhere, it would remain a mystery forever.

Shaking her head to help her put the ideas in order, Eileen stepped back and positioned herself by the two boxes that contained nothing else than old photos from her parents. She looked at them, filled her lungs, and let the air flow out slowly before kneeling in between the two of them. From what she remembered, one of the boxes contained loads of photo albums, whilst the other one had a mixture of photo albums and framed photos. On the outside however, they looked the same, so she decided to open the one that was on her left.

'*Damn it!*' she voicelessly exclaimed when she opened the box and found the spine of eight photo albums. She had spent endless hours looking at the photos they contained when she was a kid, so she could create some memories of her parents. Those memories were not like her friends', but she felt them as tangible, for they were the only ones she had.

Restraining the desire to surf those old photos once again, she flipped the box edges close, and turned to open the box on her right. When she opened it, she could not stop butterflies from coming to her stomach, yet she played as calm as all her willpower allowed her to. She did not want her grandparents to notice how broken she was feeling inside.

There were frames of very different sizes inside that box. Some of them contained just one photo, whilst others had collages of six to ten photos of people her mother had once befriended. Most of the people whose young faces had been forever preserved in those photos were complete strangers to Eileen. Could any of those be Klara Herrmann? Now that she knew that her grandmother had had a twin sister, maybe she could spot a similarity that she had not paid any attention to before.

'If ye bring the box closer to us, we could help ye,' said Leagsaidh all of a sudden.

'I...don't take me wrong grandma, but I think I want to do this alone,' said Eileen, placing her right hand over one of the frames and looking at her grandparents. 'I think I only just begin to understand how much this means to you, but I need to do this when I'm ready. It took me a really long time to recover from the fact that my parents had died in a car crash even before I could remember them. I'm not sure I can go through these in just one day,' she added, pointing with her left hand to the box that she was about to unbox.

'If I hid it this long, it was because I did not want ye to go through all that all over again. It broke my heart how ye looked at me when I first told ye. Does it make me a bad person? Maybe it does. But God knows I did it with my best intentions.' Eileen could tell that her grandmother was trying her hardest not to cry.

'I'm not angry at you, grandma,' said Eileen. She crawled all the way from where she was to place herself right next to Leagsaidh. 'Maybe I was fifteen years ago, but I'm not now. Life was meant like this for me for a reason. I am who I am because of how you brought me up. Everything that has happened to me has moulded my personality and has made me, me. As much as sometimes I would have liked to grow up like a normal kid, with parents, and grandparents, and siblings, and aunties and uncles, etcetera, I have come to realise that that would have not made me any more normal than I am now. We all have our own battles. Yet the idealised version of ourselves that we want others to see might not be the idealised version they want to see. Our flaws make us as much as our strong points do. Exposing ourselves doesn't make us any less strong, or loveable. We are the hardest to ourselves,' she added, softly touching her grandmother's nose.

And then, they hugged each other as they had never before.

- XIV -

What laid in front of them was not any different to what they had already walked through, if we intentionally forget the footprints. They had magically appeared and disappeared in a matter of a few miles. Odd, very odd indeed.

When Nora, Gabe and Theresa reached Mark and stood right next to him, they did not know what to say. It was true they had followed the footprints until that very moment, but they had had Gabe's pendant to guide them before. If the protagonists wanted to impress the teenagers, they had achieved that. They truly did not know what to do, other than stare at each other.

'Two out of two pendants have proved useful so far,' said Nora looking down at her chest and taking the pendant into her hand. 'In my opinion, and no offences here, please,' she added, looking at Theresa, 'I think Gabe's has been more useful. The footprints were easy to spot and follow. Why did they appear though? Well, that's something I don't quite understand right now…'.

'No need to apologise. I share your thoughts,' said Theresa. She either feigned really well, or she had not felt attacked at all by Nora's latest comment. 'Yet going a bit further, I don't think they just randomly allowed us to see the footprints. Maybe they were just trying to tell us something'.

'They're good at writing. They could have filled one of the blank pages on the book instead' said Mark, pointing at Nora's backpack.

'I've got the feeling they are testing us,' said Gabe, completely ignoring what Mark had just said.

'Do you?' said Mark. Even in a two words sentence, he was able to impress his irritation.

'It's true we have been guided all the way here because of the book and the pendants, but instead of taking that as gifts, I rather think of them like challenges we have passed. We, and by we, I mostly mean my sister and Nora,' he said, pointing at the two girls with both pointing fingers, 'have completed the puzzle. We were provided with the pieces, and needless to say, that's the most important part, but putting them together takes something that shouldn't be taken for granted. We've earned the right to be here'.

'That's very sweet of you, Gabe,' said Theresa, cheered up by the praise. 'But going back to what I just said, how do you reckon that helps us now?'.

'Well... on the one hand, we have succeeded in not going back and forgetting all about this nonsense,' he said. He had been unsure to use the word nonsense, should it irritate whoever was spying them, but it had been the only word he had found to describe the situation they were in. 'I mean, we have proved we are brave!'.

'That's impressive, for sure, I'm not going to say it's not, but...,' said Nora. She had been thinking about it since Theresa had mentioned that the protagonists had wanted to show them something, yet she had restrained her until Gabe had finished talking. 'But I think the aspect that has really made us worthy of anything that might happen from now on, is the fact that we have kept to our word. We were warned even before we knew what it was all about, and yet we blindly assumed the consequences! Obviously, I'm not going to say that we have been the best throughout the whole process. Take the dinner at my grandma's for instance..., but we were trusted with this information because they knew we wouldn't disappoint them. And with that, I don't mean to lose our heads and start being careless now. But we've definitely gained their respect. I've got the feeling we are closer to unravelling this mystery than anybody has ever been. We just need to last a little bit longer'.

When she finished her monologue, she felt her cheeks reddening. She had indeed thought about how they had been chosen for that, whatever their fate was, and was determined to succeed on their endeavour. Yet she was not sure whether her grimace had accompanied her speech at all. As the chosen leader, she felt in debt with her friends to be brave and take the lead when the moment required it. But she was also feeling scared. She might have not made it as visible as Mark had, but she did not like being tricked that often.

They remained still for a couple more minutes, staring at each other in turns. And then, all of a sudden, Nora's backpack started vibrating and sending out light signals through the seams. She was of course the first one to feel the vibration, but the last to see the light that was kept captive at her back.

The moment she loosened the knot of the backpack, the book jumped out and slowly travelled its way to the ground as though mimicking a feather. Once it finished its journey, the pages were rapidly flipped until the one that contained the last letter from the protagonists was displayed. Then, the page slowly turned a handless ink started filling the page:

Dear dauntless readers,

We hope you are finding yourselves comfortable in our domains. As Theresa has told you already, we have been keeping an eye on you. (We rather use that expression than the one she used. We hope you understand the difference).

It has been ages since we last allowed anyone to penetrate this much into our fortress, so we wanted to make sure you would not get distracted. As Gabe has so well guessed, we have been challenging you. (Again, we rather nuance your statement). We understand that this nonsense *requires a lot from you, but keep on trusting us as you have done so far. We can only release the information when you are ready to handle it.*

You have had very interesting conversations. Mark, we are sorry you have not found them... appropriate? Useful? Interesting? Man, you have really gotten us there! We cannot figure you out.

And last, but not least, Nora. You have really proven why you were designated as the leader of the lot. You have a voice for your own, yet you listen to what others may say. Genuine leaders have the power to make every pawn feel important because of what they are. You seem to not only understand that the smallest of details makes a standard piece a masterpiece, but that excellence comes only through the hand that is supposed to add the detail.

As you have so well guessed (we never doubted you would not), the scrawls were not meaningless. But it was not because we did not make them meaningless. You did. You all had it within you. We just (Gabe, let us use your expression here, we did like it) laid the right pieces for you to mount the puzzle. The credit is on you.

It is true that you never had an option to leave, but as Nora said, you are people of your word. You were chosen for this venture because you showed the right skills. We never moulded you; you were already special on your own.

With all that said, please, we remind you to not be desperate. Our paths will cross at some point. You just need to keep on a little bit further.

Yours sincerely,

The protagonists.

15

Eileen let softly go of Leagsaidh. The hug she had shared with her grandmother had just taught her why she had never been as close to her grandmother as she had been to her grandfather. Unfortunately for the three of them, Leagsaidh had carried such a heavy burden over her shoulders, that it had ended up drowning her capability to show vulnerability.

'Am I being too selfish wanting to do this by myself?' Eileen voicelessly asked herself while walking back to the boxes she was about to start searching into. Not wanting that doubt to occupy all her thoughts, she turned around and asked her grandparents. She did not want to have second thoughts about the whole situation.

'Each of us deals with ou' inner battles the best we can, the way we can. Neither I'm the one to tell ye how to do it, nor I think there's anybody who can. Fer sure, ye can get guided towards how to do things, but it's only ye who makes the decisions,' said Alick. That had not been the reply Eileen had searched for, but she understood what her grandfather meant. Or at least she thought she did.

She had felt her inner hope fire intensified by the sudden discovery of Klara Herrmann's full name. Nonetheless, and as much as she wanted to remain sensible, she could not help imagining the scenario she wanted their whereabouts turned into. She was aware of the battle between her rational and not-so-rational inner selves, and although she wanted to bet all for one, her instinct told her that was the riskiest of all bets. And that left her empty inside, for her instinct had never failed her.

Nodding her head thanks to her grandfather, Eileen turned around and sat by the boxes that read 'Nora & Aksel. Photos 1' and 'Nora & Aksel. Photos 2'. She had decided to first go through the frames, so she reopened the box and took one without looking at the photo. Before dismounting it however, she turned it around. It contained a photo of a young Nora, who seemed to have been having a lot of fun while in the mountains, as regarded the big smile her mouth was drawing. Behind her, there was a wooden cottage that sounded somehow familiar to Eileen. She stared at it until she blinked her eyes, and a tear dropped onto the glass that protected the photo. Cleaning away another tear with her sleeve, she then turned the frame and began dismounting it.

Once the four thumbtacks were laying on the floor, she carefully removed the cork they had been attached to and was not surprised to find a small piece of paper hiding between it and the back of the photography. It was roughly of the same size as the one she had discovered hidden on the frame from the photo that had hung on her wall:

Trip to Finland, 1986. After a beautiful hiking route and once back in the cottage, Aksel proposed. He had been acting weird, but I had not been able to figure it out. I can't believe I'm marrying the love of my life!

Once she read the caption, Eileen realised why the cottage had sounded so familiar: one of the albums contained a whole lot of pages with photos her parents had taken during that trip. Yet what made her feel the most emotional was the fact that maybe her grandmother was right, and they could be able to find useful information hidden in the frames.

She looked back to tell her grandparents, but they were nowhere to be found. They had left her alone in the living room. Thus, she turned to look back at the boxes and, as smoothly as she could, she said: 'Please mum, guide me on this'.

She then took another frame and repeated the same process. Once she turned it around, she found a group of young men and women who had just finished university. They were all wearing graduating gowns and were looking upside to the hats they had just thrown into the air. She then turned it around, removed the thumbtacks and the cork, and found a small piece of paper lying on the back of the photo:

> *Salzburg, 1985. Aksel's graduation. I would have made it if only I had not failed that Physics exam and had had to resit it. He was always the cleverest of the couple.*

Eileen left the frame upside down right next to the one she had dismounted first and placed the small piece of paper on top of the previous one. She had no idea where her grandparents had gone, but she was determined to show them everything she found out. She then continued dismounting frames and collecting the pieces of paper that her mother had once hidden behind the photos.

> *Pitlochry, 1989. Germany might be where my house is, but Scotland will always be home. Trip before giving birth to Eileen, who undoubtedly will be Scottish born.*

> *Hamburg, 1984. Dinner at Michael's. From left to right: Michael, Ulrike, me, Aksel, Matthias, Lukas and Lena.*

Glasgow, 1981. My first dorm as a university student! It doesn't look too cosy, but I'll do my best.

Eileen kept on dismounting frames until she read the caption that had been hidden behind a photo of her parents and her Austrian grandparents:

Salzburg, 1986. Trip to visit my in-laws to tell them the good news! Aksel's friends were also around. What a welcoming country Austria is.

She reread it and looked closely at the photo thrice before standing up. It could not be true! Trying to remain sensible however, she kneeled next to the frame, took the photo and had yet another close look at it. That person whose reflection was on the mirror... that had to be Klara! Her hair looked different, but her face... it was a younger version of her grandmother's.

Eileen's heartbeat had arisen inevitably when she had recognised Klara's face on the reflection. Before telling her grandparents however, she decided to have a look at the photo albums, to see whether her mother had also captioned the photos she had not considered that important as to be placed on frames. Thus, she opened the other box and read the spines of the photo albums until she found the one she had been looking for: '1986 -Nora & Aksel'.

The fact that her mother had been so thorough on her memories keeping had helped her in her own memories creation process. As a kid, she had studied every single photo and had not passed to the next page until she had been able to remember the story she had created from the graphical memories her parents had left behind and the stories her grandparents had told her. For that reason, she perfectly remembered that there were two pages full of photos from that day.

Eileen flipped the pages as fast as she could until she got to the photos she had been looking for. Klara seemed to not be on any of them, but knowing as she did that her great aunt had indeed been in that celebration, Eileen took a closer look at the photos where the mirror was visible. There was someone reflected on those photos as well, although it was fainter than it had been on the photo that had been selected to be on the frame. Could have that been coincidental? Leaving the assumptions making aside however, she introduced her finger in between the photo and the plastic from the photo-holding folder and smiled widely when her finger sensed a piece of paper.

- XV -

Once Nora finished reading the latest letter from the protagonists, she handed the book to Theresa and sat down. Her face had gone completely pale, and rather than having a scene should she faint, she had decided to sit down first. With her eyesight lost far away between the trees, it took her a while to realise that Theresa was talking to her.

'Nora, are you alright?' repeated Theresa for the fifth time. 'Please, do say something! This is scary enough as it is…'.

'So… sorry,' said Nora, shaking her head and then looking at Theresa. 'I'm ok. It's just that, well, I knew they knew our names, but I wasn't expecting them to be addressing us directly. And the fact that they knew what we had talked about… I guess you get my point, don't you?'.

'I do indeed.' Theresa closed the book and sat down right in front of Nora. 'Me on the contrary, I was expecting something to happen. Maybe not this,' she added, pointing at the book, 'but something at the end of the day. You've said it before: we are closer than anybody has ever been to unravel the mystery!'.

'So?' Nora did not want to be rude, but as she had been completely taken aback, she could not word her feelings correctly. She did not know what to think or what to do other than stare at Theresa and hope for her to find a way out.

'Look over there,' was all Theresa said while stretching her right hand and pointing it towards the trees that laid right in front of them.

Nora looked at Theresa as though her friend had gone mad, for she was widely smiling. But when she looked towards where Theresa was pointing at, she realised why she was smiling: not far from where they were standing, the trees suddenly became smaller and less dense. And… if she forced her eyes to see the details… was that even possible? Was that what she wanted it to be?

As an instinct reaction, Nora stood up, leaving her backpack next to Theresa, and ran past a couple of trees. Mark followed her, and when he reached her, he looked back at where the twins were standing and smiled widely, too. When he realised that Gabe was pointing at him, he looked down at his chest and saw that his pendant had come to life. After their long walk through the forest, they had eventually found the monster's dwelling.

'Guys, let's go! C'mon! Stand up! We've got some caves to explore!' exclaimed Mark, all excited. He ran back to help Theresa pick up the book and Nora's backpack and ran again all the way to where Nora had been to give her back her belongings.

'Calm down, dude. Don't make me wish for the old Mark to be back,' said Gabe, laughing.

Nora took the backpack Mark was offering her, as well as the book, although she decided to not put it back inside, and rather keep it in her hand. She then turned around and looked ahead. They did not have a long walk until they reached the caves, and the forest seemed to be summoned in the same peaceful atmosphere as it had for as long as they had been inside it. Nevertheless, she could not help feeling uneasy about the whole situation. All that quietness made her think that something strange would be happening soon.

With Mark on the lead, the four teenagers resumed their walk towards the centre of the forest itself. His pendant had started signing brighter and brighter as they were getting closer to their destination. Gabe and Theresa's had also recovered their glow, although they were not as bright as Mark's. As for Nora's however, it looked like an ordinary pendant without any magical powers whatsoever.

'Your turn will come. Don't be desperate,' said Gabe. Nora had been so busy with her daydreaming, that she had not realised that Gabe had found his way towards her side.

'It's not about the pendant, or at least not solely about it,' said Nora while unconsciously playing with the pendant. 'The thing is, I'm used to preparing everything thoroughly beforehand, so the fact that I don't know what we will face when we get there is making me quite nervous. Does it make any sense to you?'.

'It is completely normal that we feel afraid of the unknown. And trust me, it is the same for all of us,' said Gabe, circling his hand to point at his sister, Mark and himself. 'Look at Mark for instance, he had been really annoying for the whole journey and suddenly, something inside of him changed. When we're nervous we do things that we would not dare to otherwise, but isn't that what spices up our lives?'.

'But his change has been for the good. What about me becoming a failure as a leader? I've just got the feeling I've been given a task for which I have not been trained for, so it could be that I don't succeed. I just don't want to let you down,' said Nora, feeling completely crestfallen. She was not very good at talking about her feelings with anyone, but she felt comfortable doing so with Gabe. He had something that made her trust him.

'For the good? He's just become annoying in a different way!' exclaimed Gabe in laughs. He then took his eyes off Nora and looked forward to where Mark was. He was still on the lead, using his pendant as a compass. Nora did not quite understand why he was doing that, as its brightness did not seem to be altered at all depending on where he pointed it at. Giggling at the sight, Nora looked back at Gabe, who resumed: 'About you... well, I've already told you: I don't think there is a head cleverer than yours here. No please, let me finish' said Gabe when he realised Nora was about to reply. 'I bet that once or twice, if not more, something has gone wrong during one of your auditions, yet I don't recall my grandmother saying that you had been on the news for that. On the contrary, every time I've heard of you before we met it was because you were praised, widely praised I mean. Nora, you are just 16 and you are world-famous for what you do! Have you got any idea how many people would like to be on your feet? You've got the talent and the discipline. You're worth every single thing that happens to you'.

Gabe's confession left Nora speechless. She truly did not know what to say back, so she decided to say nothing at all. She did not consider herself lucky for what she had, as she had not gotten anything for granted. She did feel pleased however, but that was a completely different feeling. It was true that she had been gifted the ability to understand music from a very young age, but should it had not been for her parents, her grandmother Mary and Mr Ross, she would have never achieved anything of what she had. She was extremely good at playing the piano, but she was not that good a handling stressful situations.

A few months after she had moved to London to take piano lessons with Mr Ross, she had had an audition at the Shakespeare's Globe. She had practised her performances thousands of times, yet she had been completely unable to stop her from feeling unprepared for the occasion. That day, only five students from her music school were performing. Tickets had sold out within hours, and chancellors from different institutions were attending. The pressure had been real.

After school, her father had picked her up and had driven her to the theatre. On their way in the car, neither of them had talked. Nora had been really busy revising her scores, and her father had had to keep really focused on the road, as the traffic had seemed to go wild that evening. Once they had reached their destination, Nora had kissed her father goodbye and had entered the theatre from the back. She had been feeling so nervous, that she had not realised she had left her backpack with her scores in the backseat. So naturally, by the moment she had realised that, she had started panicking.

Mr Ross had been extremely nice and welcoming to her, so she had practised more than she had ever before in order to not disappoint him. Thus, when she had realised she did not have her partitures with her, she had run to where the caretakers were and had begged to borrow the telephone. She knew her parents' phone numbers by heart, so she dialled them. She first tried with her father, wishing that he was still around the area, and could come back and give her the scores. On the fifth tone however, she realised he was not to be reached, and therefore hanged up and tried with her mother.

She had clung to the phone tighter with every tone, but her mother had not answered the phone either. She had felt alone, frightened and sad. But as smart as she was, she had realised that staying by the phone would not be of any help to her, so she had turned around, had thanked the caretakers and had gone back to her dressing room to wait for Mr Ross. About ten minutes later, which seemed like hours to Nora, Mr Ross entered her dressing room. He was a very cheerful man, but his whole joy had left him the moment he had realised Nora, who was sitting on the couch, had been crying.

'What's wrong, Nora?' he had said, slowly coming closer to the couch and kneeling right in front of her.

'I...I'v...I've leeeeeft my...mmy...scooo...res. I'm...I'm sss...so...sorry,' had said Nora, sobbing.

'I'm sure we could arrange that. I could get hold of some spare copies,' had said Mr Ross. As he was used to working with kids, he had always been prepared for their slips. Dealing with psychology however, that was something that he had never felt comfortable with, although he had always tried his best. 'Although I don't think you are a musician who can't perform without a score. You're one of a kind, Nora. I haven't seen a talent like yours in such a small body before. When I contacted your parents, I did so because I knew we could make great things together.

»Growing up I dreamed of becoming a world-renowned pianist. Every time I had a couple of spare hours, I would either play the piano or compose new music. I was a geek, I can't say I was not, but unfortunately many people only cared about that. Yet I was never ashamed of what I was. I wouldn't listen to the people that said I would never earn a living like that. I've clearly proved them wrong'.

'But you aren't known for your music. You're known for your pupils,' had said Nora.

'Bless your honesty!' had exclaimed Mr Ross in laughs. 'Although, yes, I am indeed. But I don't feel like a failure: I've got everything I've ever wanted. I might have not become the person I dreamed of becoming, but I do feel I am the person I needed when I was a kid. And that fills my heart. Even though I dreamed of it, I was never meant to travel the world to play in the most important theatres, but rather to assist those playing. Every single artist needs a good mentor who supports them and cheers them up whenever they feel their world is upon them. I'm the one who will share his secrets with you, so that you become a successful person. Thus, are you ready for my first secret?'.

Mr Ross had been unable to stop from giggling because of how enthusiastic Nora had become. The sadness that had overcome her only a few minutes before had left as suddenly as it had come. 'Kids' had thought Mr Ross before looking back at Nora and adding: 'It's okay to have doubts and fears; it shows that we respect what's ahead. What is not that okay is that we doubt of our own capabilities. We are the hardest to ourselves because we never stop comparing our flaws, or what we perceive as flaws, with the strong points of other people, or what we perceive as strong points anyway. Thus, whenever you find yourself in a self-doubt moment, close your eyes, hold your hands together, and say: I will enjoy the journey and I will learn from my mistakes, for I am worthy of the trust of others'.

- 16 -

Salzburg, 1986. Trip to visit my in-laws to tell them the good news! Klara Herrmann (Aksel's first primary school teacher) refused to be in the photo, but she joined the celebration. Her husband, Leon Herrmann, and their kids, Matthias, Lukas and Sandra, also joined our celebration. This was the private celebration of our engagement; we celebrated it further with Aksel's friends.

Eileen had to read the caption five times before she was able to understand it. The moment her finger had sensed the piece of paper hidden behind the photo, her heartbeat had arisen. Although it had not been anything compared to how fast it had beaten when her eyes had glimpsed Klara Herrmann's name. She had somehow wished for that information to be on the caption, yet the fact that she was being so lucky had taken her completely unprepared.

'Grandpa! Grandma! Where are you? I've got something to show you,' shouted Eileen, standing up. She had not realised how much time she had spent sitting in the same position, but her body punished her for not having moved with a numbing sensation in her legs. *'Not even this will stop me from getting to the end,'* thought Eileen, bending and stretching her legs before taking the papers she had stacked.

Her grandparents had not replied to her shouting, which she found quite odd, so Eileen considered the possibility they were at the backyard, enjoying the sunny weather. When she went outside however, she could not find them there either. *'Where the hell are they?'* asked Eileen to herself while turning around and going inside again. She then went back to the living room, for that was the only way to go to the front door. Although when she was about to open the front door, she heard voices upstairs. With a big smile on her face, she removed her shoes and ran up the stairs jumping two steps at a time.

Before reaching the door of the living room upstairs, Eileen eavesdropped her grandfather comforting her grandmother. The smile she had worn on her face since she had discovered where her grandparents were, left her to be substituted by a concerned look. Taking a few deep breathes, she knocked on the door and went inside.

'Is everything alright, grandma?' asked Eileen while hiding in her jeans pocket the pieces of paper she had brought with her.

Leagsaidh tried to explain herself, but every time she tried to say anything, her sobs became louder, so Alick placed his hand over his wife's, caressed it, and talked for her instead: 'It's just been too much fer her. Both ye and I have discovered a part of her story we have neve' heard of before, and that's been shocking. So if it's been tough fer ye and I, imagine how it's been fer her. I'm afraid we can't ask her fer anything more than she's done already. Should she want us to stop 'ight now, then that's what we shall do. Understood?'.

Eileen did not remember her grandfather ever being that tough on her, and that took her aback. Naturally, she had been told off as a kid, but she did not recall him going that serious about anything. Not even that one time when she had crashed their old television when practising her karate movements at home. Her grandmother had however gone ballistic about it. But, for the time being, their roles seemed to have swapped.

Not knowing what to say, Eileen looked from her grandfather to her grandmother, and then back to her grandfather. Leagsaidh continued crying, although she slowly seemed to be regaining her breath. As for Alick, his serious grimace did not match the look in his eyes. He was trying really hard to be imposing, but as that was not on his nature, Eileen sought for the papers in her jeans' pocket and handed them to him without further ado.

An unconscious smile appeared on Alick's face before he turned his head to look at his wife. Leagsaidh had her head hidden behind her hands, so he assumed she had not seen anything, and thus turned back to look at Eileen, offer his hand to her, and take the papers she was offering him. Using his body as a shield, he started unfolding the papers and reading them.

That had not been the way Eileen had thought of telling her grandparents that they were closer than ever to discover what had been of Klara (or Clarissa) after all those years, but she decided to embrace the moment anyway. Maybe, and just maybe, should her grandmother read the papers, they would be willing to track Klara down. Maybe, and just maybe, they would be able to reunite the siblings again.

When Alick reached the last piece of paper, he could not help but smile widely. Nevertheless, when Leagsaidh moaned, he was startled and all the pieces of paper he had kept on his lap fell on the floor, where they were visible to his wife.

'Whaaat...r...rr...thoooose?' asked Leagsaidh, wiping her wet cheeks with the back of her sleeve.

Eileen looked apologetically at her grandfather and then said: 'Your sister changed her name to Klara Herrmann. She married Leon and had three kids: Matthias, Lukas and Sandra. It's all here,' she added, giving the biggest piece of paper to her grandmother for her to read it.

Leagsaidh offered a trembling hand to Eileen, who placed the piece of paper on her hand. And, as it had happened to her, her grandmother had to reread the caption more than once for her brain to fully process every detail.

'Are ye serious?' was all Leagsaidh said. She did not cry, neither got angry nor showed any other emotion. She just acted as nothing had happened at all.

'Of course I am, grandma. Why would I not anyway?' said Eileen. Given her grandmother's rollercoaster of emotions, she felt she was completely unable to predict what her next move would be.

'We don' have to do anything if ye don' want to, Leagsaidh. Eileen will understand it, and so will I,' said Alick. He was also feeling unsafe for his wife's reactions.

'Don' take my moment of vacillation as the answer fer eve'ything, Alick,' said Leagsaidh. Again, she sounded neither angry nor afraid, yet her words made both Eileen and her grandfather feel uneasy. 'I much appreciate yer worrying fer me, but I decided I was in when I shared with ye both my story. Nonetheless, that does not mean I won't have moments of self-doubt. Ye've no idea how many times I've dreamed of having the opportunity to face my sister again and ask her eve'ything that has prevented me frem living a happily-ever-after life. I wonder whether she ever grieved our father or Balthair, or whether she ever really cared 'bout me. I still don't know whether I will get the answers to all my questions, but...'.

'But you're more afraid of actually getting them, than not at all,' interrupted Eileen. Her grandmother had no idea how much she related to her on that.

'*I will enjoy the journey and I will learn from my mistakes, for I am worthy of the trust of others. I will enjoy the journey and I will learn from my mistakes, for I am worthy of the trust of others. I will...,*' repeated Nora in her head, with her eyes closed and her hands held together until Mark startled her with a scream: 'what happened?' she said, opening her eyes.

'How could I be so stupid? Of course, it was not going to be that easy!' exclaimed Mark, turning around. Since his pendant had started glowing, he had walked a few steps ahead of the other three, so he had to shout for them to clearly hear him.

'Dude, calm down,' said Gabe, putting all his effort into not laughing. Mark acting motivated about their adventure had been a really good delusion. 'What's wrong?'.

'There isn't just one cave, but four. Four! How are we supposed to know which one is the correct one?' said Mark. He had not been able to wait for his friends to reach the end of the path. His small patience had made him decide to walk towards them instead.

'Ooh, that!' exclaimed Gabe. This time he could not hold himself and started laughing. Theresa looked at him disapprovingly before starting talking.

'Maybe the four of them are the correct ones. Four caves, four people,' she said, pointing with one hand ahead, to where the caves were, and to Nora, her brother, Mark and herself with the other one. 'Notwithstanding, I would not worry too much about that just yet. We've been guided so far, and I've no doubt we will still be guided. It'll either be through the pendants, the book, or them showing up here, but

I've no doubt we will get notified of what move we should make next. Just calm down. Everything will be sorted out'.

Mark looked at Theresa as though she had gone completely mad, and that made Nora laugh in her insides. She was having the impression that every time that Theresa had told them something, they had all looked at her as though something was not working in her brains. The truth was however, that she had always seemed to be one step ahead of them all. She clearly had no idea how much Nora envied her for that.

Nora had found Mr Ross's secrets very helpful, not only for her musical preparation but for her life in general. She had unconsciously integrated his methods into her daily life whenever she had felt stressed, or overwhelmed, or even sad. And as much as she had been able to control her emotions then, she was not finding it that easy with her current emotional rollercoaster. She was not able to name what was it that she was feeling, as she was having too many emotions at the same time.

She had been able to tell Gabe about her fear of failure, but that was not the only fear she had experienced during their journey. To start with, she had found it hard to believe that magic existed, but her willingness to get to the end of all matters had balanced everything in favour of her exploring half. Coming closer to her new friends for the dos, and the fact that her grandmother had acted so mysterious for the don'ts, had balanced one another as well. The closer they were getting to the end of their adventure, the more she felt the don'ts were going to end up winning. Nonetheless, in order not to drain into that well, she forced herself to start busying her mind with something else.

With the *All Scottish Legends* copy still in her hand, she walked past her friends and came closer to one of the caves' entrances. They had been completely unaware that, during their walk to the centre of the forest itself, they had actually climbed up a hill. It had been such a gradual ascension, and they had been so absorbed in their whereabouts, that she had not realised that until they had reached the caves. However, from the clearing where the entrances were, the slope did become more noticeable.

With her free hand, Nora explored the silhouette of the entrance to one of the caves. The rock had some patches of moss here and there, but for most of it, it remained very clear. Just as though somebody had been taking care of it, so it did not look too wild. What took her attention however was not the neatness of the surface, but something that seemed to have been engraved onto it. She first gave it a close look and then decided to pass her fingers over the outline.

The moment her fingers touched the centre of the engraving, she felt her pendant vibrating for just a split second. Or maybe it kept vibrating for longer, but she was not aware of it, as she turned around and focused on what Mark was yelling:

'My pendant is vibrating! My pendant is vibrating!' he kept repeating. Despite his late leadership, he had not moved far from where the clearing and the path became one.

'I told you we were going to be guided,' said Theresa, coming closer to him. 'All we have to do now is discover how to take leverage from it. What do your guts tell you?'.

'My guts tell me to go back to my grandmother's,' replied Mark, ironically. 'But I can't do that. *They* won't allow it, and I wouldn't let you all by yourselves here. As your brother would say, I've come to my senses,' he added, looking at Gabe.

'Indeed mate! Better late than never,' said Gabe, patting his friend softly. Turning his head towards where Nora was, he added: 'What do your guts tell you, leader?'.

'Enough with the fun, Gabe,' said Theresa, clearly angry at her brother for his latest comment. 'You're to respectfully treat her. Despite you not seeing it, we are being watched, and that rudeness of yours won't get us anywhere good. So, if you please, could we concentrate on figuring out how to use Mark's pendant?'.

Gabe apologetically looked at Nora. She had appreciated the sense that Gabe had tried to impose onto his question, although she agreed with Theresa that the wording had not been very wisely chosen. After accepting his silent apologies, she started talking:

'To start with, I find this clearing is very neat as to be in the middle of nowhere, so it clearly proves that it is being taken care of. Given that we are dealing with magic however, I wouldn't necessarily suggest that it is because *they* spend a lot of time doing so, although it could very well be. I don't know how much action there is in here anyway,' she said, sitting down as well. After leaving her backpack and the book in the middle of the circle, she resumed: 'Despite that neatness, what I find yet more out of place are the engravings that are by the entrance of the caves. I've only seen one closely, but I've got the feeling they are all the same. To me, they represent doorbells, but as though the button had been stuck, if you know what I mean. Does that lead your thinking in any way?'.

She only got the weird looks of her friends as a response, which made her feel uneasy again. Feeling dumb, she embraced her knees and hid her head behind them. She started daydreaming about what her friends might be thinking of her, so she did not see how Theresa seemed to have understood what she had meant.

Although it passed completely unnoticed to Nora, Gabe and Mark witnessed how Theresa left her backpack on the ground, stood up and ran towards the closest cave. Once there, she positioned herself right in front of the entrance of one of the caves and, whilst looking at her friends, she dragged her fingers over the engraving. Her contact with the rock did not last long, but it seemed to have been enough for her.

'Nora, your connection between the engravings and doorbells was indeed very accurate,' said Theresa, retaking her position. 'Although the button is not stuck, but missing. Lucky for us however, I do know where to find it. Or better said: them'.

Nora discreetly wiped some tears from her cheeks before looking back at her. She opened her mouth to reply, but Gabe was faster than her: 'Don't hold it, sis! Shed light on us'.

'The pendants!' exclaimed Mark. 'The pendants are the missing buttons. They are our way in…'.

'And your way out,' said a woman's voice that neither of them had heard ever before.

And then, all of a sudden, the pendants released from their necks and travelled to the caves. Each one of them travelled to a different cave, but they did not insert themselves into the engravings. Instead, they remained suspended in the air, right in front of where they were supposed to be inserted. Then, the same voice spoke again:

'Dear dauntless readers, here starts the beginning of the end. Please, insert your pendants in the engravings. We'll meet you shortly after that. Yours sincerely, The Protagonists'.

Hiding her fear the best she could, Nora grabbed the book to put it inside her backpack. The moment she touched it, she felt something had changed on it, and thus looked down at it. What she saw made her laugh, and before her friends were scared to death by her reaction, she said: 'Look at this'.

Gabe, Mark and Theresa crawled closer to Nora. She could not judge them for their uncertain looks. Unlike it had always happened, they had been told what would happen, rather than getting it confirmed. The book, whose cover had remained still for as long as they had had it, was now showing a moving image of four caves coming closer. They all seemed to be guided by a shining spot on the right side of their entrances, which was where the engravings on the caves that stood in front of them were.

'As always, you were right, Theresa. Four caves for four people,' said Nora while putting the book in her backpack. She had not followed her pendant, but she somehow felt as though they would not choose incorrectly. Once the other three were in front of their pendants, she added: 'at the count of three. One...Two...'.

'Three!' they said all in unison.

Then, everything went dark.

17

O nce Leagsaidh recomposed, the three of them decided to go back to the living room to keep on looking for possibly useful information. It was true they had enough for Eileen to start filtering on social media, but should they find anything else, that task would be completed much faster.

'Which was the photo that kept the caption hidden?' asked Leagsaidh when she retook her seat.

'I...let me see,' said Eileen. She had been so excited about the finding of the piece of paper, that she had not paid any attention to the photo itself. Thus, she walked past the armchairs and kneeled in front of the one photo album that had remained open.

All the photos on the two pages were very similar to one another. They had all been taken in front of a photocall that claimed '*Mann und Frau zu sein*'. And, in all of them, Nora and Aksel had been joined by their family and friends. She had found the paper hidden behind the photo that had had the most people posing for it. As it had been for the rest of the photos, Nora and Aksel were happily smiling in the centre of the photocall, with their hands raised to point at the words *Mann* and *Frau*. Their companions, Aksel's parents, and who Eileen recognised as Leon and his kids, were all pointing at the words *zu sein*. Having a closer look, she also recognised Klara on the reflection in the mirror. That made her tenderly smile before handing the photo to her grandmother.

'Maybe I never wanted to see it, but Sandra does look a lot like you,' said Eileen, sitting down on the floor, right in front of her grandparents. 'The two boys have to be Matthias and Lukas, and the old man that's not my grandpa, that's gotta be Leon. And... well, my mum wasn't completely right about

Klar…Clarissa not being in the photo. If you look at the reflection on the mirror, you'll be able to see her'.

'This boy is a vivid rec'eation of his father when he was younger,' said Leagsaidh pointing at either Matthias or Lukas, no one knew. 'And yes, I guess Sandra does look like her mother. I wonder though why Clarissa didn't want to be in the photo'.

'Maybe she was neve' honest 'bout her past,' ventured Alick. 'I mean, we know that, at some point, she did open 'bout her roots, but that doesn't necessarily mean that she told Nora that she was her aunt. Or maybe she neve' knew, although I doubt it, to be honest'.

'Why so, grandpa?' asked Eileen.

'Even people that refuse to be taken photos forget about that condition when they're overjoyed. In such situations, it takes a great deal of self-control to keep up with the role-keeping, so mistakes are made. Should Clarissa have known 'bout the reflection of the mirror being on camera, she would have left the room while the photoshoot. I do not doubt that. But she did not leave, fer she didn't want to miss the celebration. At the end of the day, that was the closest she'd be to the wedding itself'.

'Did any of them fly over for the wedding?' asked Eileen pointing at the photo that her grandmother was still holding.

'The'e were a lot of friends frem yer parents whom we did not know, but I don't recall any of these faces,' said Leagsaidh. 'Although it was a long time ago, and my memo'y isn't what it used to be…'.

'Fair enough,' said Eileen, calmly. Since her grandfather had suggested that Klara Herrmann had not been honest with her parents, she had started thinking about the other possibility: that her parents had never been honest about them not knowing the family connections that Nora and Aksel's first primary school teacher shared. While listening to her grandparents, Eileen had pondered the possibility of not suggesting such a controversial approach, but she declined not asking. They had to be opened to all possibilities, should they want to find out the truth: 'So... I was thinking... could had it been that my parents actually knew, but decided to never share it with you?'.

To her surprise however, neither of her grandparents seemed to have felt uneasy about the question.

'We neve' taught Nora that way, but who knows. We can't be sure she neve' knew, and we've got no way to ask her now,' said Alick. Eileen wondered whether her grandfather had wanted to sound as sad as he had, but before she was done with her inner questioning, her grandmother took over:

'As someone who's hidden a huge secret fer a really long time, I can say that I neve' saw any sign that suggested that Nora was hiding anything frem us. She was always a ve'y warm and close daughter to us. On the contrary howeve', we only got to see her eve'y so often after she met Clarissa fer the first time. After her exchange year, she came back to Glasgow to finish up her degree and once done, she moved back to Germany. It's much easier to pretend when on a phone call. I... I truly don't want to doubt of my own daughter, but I can't be sure of anything anymore'.

'Oooh, grandma!' When Leagsaidh started crying again, Eileen stood up and went to where her grandmother was to hug her. She had not pretended her questioning to make her cry again, yet she did not know what to say back. Given the emotional status of her grandmother, anything that Eileen could say could be completely misunderstood, so she decided to say nothing at all.

Eileen hugged her grandmother for a few minutes before pulling away to keep on with her research. She had had an idea that could be the last tip she needed to eventually find a way to contact her great aunt. She just needed to ask the questions to the one and only person that knew the answers: her mother.

Wishing for her hypothesis to be true, Eileen kneeled again in front of the opened boxes and dug for the photo album from the wedding. It did not take her long to find it, as it was, by far, the thickest of them all. Once she had the photo album in her hands, she opened it on the first page. It showed a full-length page photo of her parents that Eileen stared at for a few seconds before slowly introducing her hand in between the photo and the folder. And, as it had happened with the rest of the photos, she did find something hidden behind it. That time however, she did not just sense a small piece of paper, but also an envelope. And, although she knew she would not find anything that she did not know already, she decided to pull the caption first:

Pitlochry, 1987. Mr and Mrs Häusler! Although I chose to keep my maiden name, that day I confirmed that I belonged with Aksel and nobody else. What a wonderful day it was. The hiccups we had during the preparation were all worth it when I saw him in his wedding suit. He couldn't hold his tears when he saw me walking the aisle with my father, but he wasn't the only one. I would have run to hug and comfort him, but I was having trouble with just walking; my legs felt like jelly. Ooh Aksel, how lucky I was to find you. Ich liebte, und liebe, und werde dich immer von ganzem Herzen lieben.

Once she finished reading the caption, she carefully put it back in the folder and took over the envelope. The moment she was able to read what was written on the outside, she lost her breath for a second: the letter had been addressed by no other than Klara Herrmann! With a trembling hand, she opened the envelope and started reading:

Liebes Paar,

Ich bin so glücklich, dass ihr meine Familie und mich zu eurer Hochzeit eingeladen habt. Leider fürchte ich, dass ich es nicht schaffen werden. Obwohl ein Teil der Familie kommen wird: Matthias, Lukas und Sandra werden es schaffen. Und obwohl ich zum genannten Datum nicht dabei sein werde, wollte ich dir ein kleines Geschenk schicken.

Ich wurde mit klassischer Musik vertraut gemacht, als ich meinen jetzigen Mann kennenlernte. Er hat mir alles beigebracht, was ich über Bach, Mozart und Beethoven weiß. Als Kind bekam ich nie die Gelegenheit, ihnen zuzuhören, aber als ich ihn traf, öffnete er eine Tür voller neuer Möglichkeiten.

Seitdem vergeht kein Tag mehr, an dem ich mir keines seiner Stücke anhöre. Deshalb kaufte ich Ihnen eine Zusammenstellung ihrer Werke. Meine Kinder denken, dass ich Ihnen das nicht vorschlagen sollte, aber ich habe mich gefragt, ob Sie den Gang zu Beethovens sechster Symphonie gehen würden. Es ist bei weitem das Lieblingslied von Leon und mir, also dachten wir, das könnte die Art sein, wie wir bei Ihnen sein können, ohne dabei körperlich anwesend zu sein.

Es tut mir so leid, dass wir nicht bei Ihnen sein werden. Ich hoffe, Sie können uns vergeben.

Deine Klara.

Eileen suppressed with all her will the tears that were coming to her eyes. Leaving the letter on the floor, she went to the desktop where her grandfather kept her old computer and turned it on. After what seemed like an eternity to her, she was able to click on the Google Chrome icon and type 'The Sixth symphony, by Beethoven'. She then chose the first link and, once the speakers started working, she turned around and asked:

'Is this the song my mum walked the aisle to?'.

'It is indeed. Why?' said Alick, not understanding what was going on.

- XVII -

'**A**re you guys alright?' asked Nora when she felt her pendant hanging from her neck again. She could not see anything, as they were still embraced by thick darkness, so she did not dare move. Despite that however, she needed to hear from her friends.

'I am, I guess,' said Mark. His voice was tinged with a genuine fear that made Nora feel pity for him. If only she had known where he was, she would have hugged him to comfort him.

'Same here,' said Gabe. None could see each other, but should they have, they would have laughed at how Gabe was moving his arms. He was making a windmill as though that would protect him in any way.

'Aaaaaaaah!' screamed Theresa.

'Aaaaaaaaaaaaaaah!' screamed Gabe. 'What the f...!'.

'Don't you dare, Gabe!' said Theresa. 'Nothing of this would have happened SHOULD YOU HAVE REMAINED STILL! What were you thinking? You hit my back really bad'.

'I'm sorry, sis. I panicked and that...well...I was trying to protect myself and I... I accidentally hit you. I didn't mean to'.

'Anyways, Gabe. Did walking while moving your arms seem like the best way to protect yourself? Didn't your brains tell you that if you can't see you may as well fall? You're lucky you hit me and not somebody else. We don't even know whether we're alone in here. We need to remain sensible about the whole situation and not make any stupid movements. We're so close to unravelling the mystery...

don't mess it up, please,' begged Theresa, who was still rubbing her back, right where her brother had hit her.

Nora was about to reply that they should stop arguing when the darkness that had filled the room they were in was suddenly replaced by an extremely bright light. It was such a bright light indeed, that it was painful to their eyes, as they were already used to the darkness. Thus, not only did they close their eyes, but they also felt the need to cover them with their hands.

The four teenagers remained in that position for about a minute, until their eyes got used to the brightness that prevailed now in the room. A minute that for them was as though time had stopped, but that had been leveraged by their hosts. The protagonists had walked into the room through the only corridor that gave access to it and had been waiting for their visitors to regain the power of their eyesight.

'Dear dauntless readers, we are very pleased to welcome you to our dwelling. We hope that, despite the circumstances, you have had a good time while hiking through our domains. We assure you that it has loads to offer to visitors, and especially, to visitors as special as yourselves. But first, let's show some manners, shall we not? Let's begin with the introductions. My name is Maia, and I'm the oldest of the lot,' she said, pointing first at herself, and then at her comrades. 'And these are my brother Nor, Cynthia, Andreas and Francesco,' she added, changing the direction of her finger as she named a new person.

'Hello there,' said the other four. They then looked back at Maia as though they would not dare do anything without her approval.

'I assume you've got loads of questions to ask us. It's normal, and don't worry, you'll get them answered at the due moment. But first, let's get moving. The clearing will appear soon, and it's better we're not here when that happens,' said

Maia while turning around. She had already started walking when Mark decided to disobey her and ask:

'How come it's better if we're not here when the caves go back to their former position? What do you mean by that?' Nora and Theresa looked at Mark as though he had gone completely insane. Had he not seen how the other four protagonists had only done as Maia had ordered? How did he dare talk when not summoned to do so?

'Their former position. That's a very interesting appreciation, honey,' said Maia without turning around. Her voice had sounded neutral, but Nora had witnessed how under her clothing, her muscles had tensed as soon as she had heard Mark talking. She was clearly not used to being contradicted.

'Would you...Aaah! No, Gabe, stop!' exclaimed Mark when Gabe nudged him on his ribs. 'I'm just trying to have a conversation with our hosts. What's so wrong about it?'.

'Hasn't Abby taught you to do as you were told? Oh yes, I do know your grandmothers. Why do you act so surprised though? I thought you've guessed that by now,' said Maia. She had not had to look back at the four teenagers to realise how her latest comment had made them feel. 'Anyways, let's keep walking. We really need to get going'.

Nora, Theresa and Gabe had panicked at the mention of the connection Maia had with their grandmothers, but it had been nothing compared to how Mark had felt when the leader of the protagonists had named her grandmother Abby. He had been so eager to reply, to get her to talk, that he had been caught with his mouth opened, and like that he had remained. He had remained that still in fact, that the only thing that proved that he was still alive was the movement of his chest as he breathed. His mouth was fully open, as well as his eyes, and he would not move.

'C'mon, Mark. We're here to support each other. We won't let anything bad happen to you,' said Nora. She had waited for their hosts to walk a little bit further into the corridor to come closer to her friend and talk to him. She doubted that would have prevented them from hearing whatever she had to say, but she had felt safer that way. 'Mark, please,' added Nora while offering her hand to him.

Although a bit reluctant at the beginning, Mark ended up taking the hand that Nora was offering him. He was shaking from head to toes, and that made Nora feel pity for him again. As afraid as she had felt at some points during their adventure, it had been nothing compared to how Mark was feeling right then. But she had to agree on the fact that the situation was weird enough for them all to feel as Mark was feeling.

It was just the four of them, without any adults or a way to contact them, inside a cave that did not feel welcoming at all. Before they had inserted their pendants in the engravings at the entrances of the caves, they had known that the caves would come together because of that and that they would be left inside the new room that would be created after their collapse. But that had been it. They had not been warned about the sudden darkness, the appearance of the protagonists, or the need to follow them through a corridor that seemed to have been handcrafted for a scary movie.

Still holding hands with Mark, Nora looked at Theresa and waited for her to say something: 'I don't know what to say. I didn't know what to expect, so I've been caught with low defences. I guess we don't have any other option but wait for them to tell us things as they deem convenient. I'm sorry,' she added, truly feeling sorry about her lack of ideas.

'You needn't feel sorry, sis. You've guided us all the way here, and I've no doubt you'll guide us out. I trust you,' said Gabe. Nora realised that he also sounded extremely scared, and that made something inside of her break apart. She needed to be brave not just for herself and Mark, but also for Gabe. Would she be able to deal with all that? She was starting to doubt it.

Not even today do they know how long did they walk for inside the cave. The path was easy to follow, as it did not have any intersections, but that did not mean it was not scary. The rock walls were plain except for a few crevices here and there, but the shadows that were originated as they walked would have scared to death even the bravest person on Earth.

And just as they were starting to desperate, Maia decided to talk again: 'We are not far from our destination. Thus, as we will shortly arrive, I'll get you a heads-up on what you will find there. I know that your grandmothers warned you to do as you were told, and even though you haven't followed the instructions strictly, you've done a pretty decent job so far. Nonetheless, as smart as you are, you will agree with me that from now on you must exactly do as you are told to. That is, if I say you don't speak, then you won't speak; if I say you cover your ears, then you cover them straight away.' She had said all that while still walking deeper inside the cave, but she turned around before asking them: 'Is that understood?'.

Mark, Theresa and Gabe hurried to nod their heads yes as soon as Maia turned around. As for Nora, she decided to hold Maia's gaze for a few seconds before daring to break the silence that had surrounded them: 'May I ask why should we do as we are told to? There has to be a reason why we have to do that. It's not that I...,' but she could not finish her sentence, for Maia interrupted her.

'COVER YOUR EARS, NOW!' had shouted Maia. Given the arrogance she had shown for as long as the teenagers had known her, her reaction had been out of the normal. 'HAVEN'T I TOLD YOU TO DO AS YOU WERE TOLD?' shouted Maia at Nora when she realised she had not followed her instructions.

'WHY?' shouted Nora back, while telling them all with her hands that they should uncover their ears. 'There is nothing wrong! It's just a melody. The same one I heard coming from my book in my bedroom,' she added, more to herself than to anybody else.

Nora could not understand why her friends were not trusting her and kept doing as they were told to. She had proved herself right so often throughout their adventure, that she was finding that behaviour insulting. Yet the fear she perceived from them through their faces… her guts told her there was something else going on. At the end of the day, neither of them had been that intentionally opened about their fear.

Tired of trying to convince them to uncover their ears, she decided to look away and carefully listen to the melody. Now that it was louder than when she had heard it coming from her *All Scottish legends* copy, she realised that it was very repetitive. As though only the same cords were being played over and over again. She closed her eyes to fully perceive the musical notes and started moving her fingers as though she was playing the piano. She remained like that for a few more minutes, until the melody started from the beginning for the sixth time, which is when she realised why the cords were so familiar to her.

She had been intrigued by the melody since she had heard it, but like it had happened when her name had been scribbled onto the book, she never thought she would be that scared to ever listen to that piece again. The last time she had listened to it, she was only a kid. She had practised it thousands of times with Mr Ross, but she had not played it since her opening at the Shakespeare's Globe exhibition. Yet what was making her feel uneasy was not that coincidence, but the fact that the melody was accompanied by some lyrics. She was unaware of that, although the more she heard the lyrics, the more she understood why she had never heard them before.

Alarmed, she turned around and started trying to catch her friends' attention again, but no matter how hard she shouted, they would not do as she was so eagerly trying them to do. Feeling the unwelcomed sensation of desperation rising, she decided to change her strategy altogether. *'They might not be able to listen to me, but they will for sure read whatever I would write,'* thought Nora while leaving her backpack on the floor and kneeling to search into it. She then pulled from it her music notebook and a pen and hurried to write a short message that read:

> *I've recognised the melody; it's the Sixth symphony, by Beethoven. Although the most important part isn't that, but the lyrics that are sung along. Uncover your ears to hear it yourselves!*

With sweaty hands, she ripped the page and positioned herself right in front of her friends for them to read her note.

'Have you gone insane?' shouted Mark when he finished reading. 'Beethoven didn't create any lyrics for his compositions. He was above all that'.

Mark, being his honest, annoying self again. Nora breathed heavily to conquer her anger and then kneeled again to write on the back of the page a reply for him:

> *I'm aware the legend dates back to a period long before Beethoven was born. And I never said he was the author of the lyrics. The melody is indeed accompanied by some vocals, but because they are so specific to our situation, I can't say which one was first.*

Regardless, the fact is they are the instructions to leave. You do need to listen to them!

Capping the pen before putting it back onto her jeans pocket, she turned around again to show the sheet of paper to Mark and whoever wanted to read it.

'NORA, WE CAN'T LISTEN TO THE MELODY BECAUSE WE AREN'T WEARING YOUR PENDANT. LOOK AT YOUR CHEST,' shouted Theresa before Mark was able to say anything else.

Nora bendt her head downwards to look at her chest, and what she saw created mixed feelings in her. Her pendant had eventually come to life, which meant her turn had arrived. And that made her feel both excited and scared. She was happy that she was going to be useful within the unravelling of the mystery, but she also felt extremely scared about the whole situation. Theresa had suggested that she was the only one able to understand the lyrics, which at the end of the day meant that their success depended on her, and only her. Would she be allowed to be helped by her companions? And why was she the only person that could understand the instructions to leave? Would they be stuck inside the cave as the protagonists if they did not succeed in their endeavours? Would she ever see her grandmother again?

18

'**B**ecause that was what Kla... Clarissa suggested she walked the aisle to. It's all in here,' said Eileen, going back to where the boxes were to take the letter she had left lying on the floor. 'Although you won't understand it, it's all written in German. If she spoke perfect English, why would she write in German every single time though?'. That was a question she had not intended to ask aloud, but when she realised she had indeed voiced it, it was already too late.

'Maybe she just wanted to make sure we wouldn't understand her letters, should we find them,' said Leagsaidh.

'Well... whatever. She changed her name! Would have you been able to track her down?' The situation was clearly getting to Eileen's nerves. There was a lot she was not understanding about the whole situation, and that was making her say things a bit more rudely than she wished she was doing. She realised that when Alick looked at her and told her off with just a flip of his eyelashes. 'And for the record, Leon and Clarissa's kids did come to the wedding. Or at least that's what she said they would do'.

'Could we all just calm down he'e?' said Alick, accommodating on his seat. 'Nobody has assured those kids were neve' around. There were many people we hadn't seen before, and that of cou'se we haven't seen eve' since. A wedding is a day fer the bride and groom, and nobody else. Regardless, I do agree with yer grandma. Even if Clarissa changed her name, she handwrote eve'y single letter, did she not? Besides, I've already told ye: I've the feeling she was neve' honest to our daughter. Is the'e anything else that she mentions in that letter?'.

'Mmmm, yes,' said Eileen, putting the letter in front of her. She then reread the letter and translated it for her grandparents. 'First of all, she thanks my parents for the invitation to the wedding, and apologizes for not being able to attend it. She however confirms that her kids would indeed attend and that she's making them a present regardless of her kids' attendance. It consists of a compilation of the songs of Bach, Mozart and Beethoven. Leon was apparently really into classical music and he introduced Clarissa to it. And well, the last bit I already told you, or at least half of it: she suggested my mum walked the aisle to Beethoven's famous Sixth symphony. It was her husband's and her favourite song, so she suggested that would be their way of being in the wedding without physically being there'.

'Oh really!?' exclaimed Leagsaidh all of a sudden. Her facial expression had completely changed from worried to sceptical.

'That's what's in here. I haven't made it up,' said Eileen, moving the letter in front of her for her grandmother to look at it. 'Is there anything else you know that you want to share with us?'.

As a reply, Leagsaidh stood up and slowly walked her way to the shelf that was next to the record player. It held dozens of vinyl records that they had used to liven up the rainy afternoons while Eileen was growing up. There were all types of music recorded on them, from Michael Jackson to Aretha Franklin, or the Rolling Stones and The Beatles. There was also some classical music, but those were rarely played because they did not have any lyrics and they had had the most fun when they organized their own karaoke. But Leagsaidh did not look for a vinyl record on display, she instead used her own pendant to open the box that was right behind the record player.

Eileen could not understand anything that was going on. To start with, she had no idea that that piece of furniture the record player had always been on had a hidden cupboard. But she had discovered quite a few things so far about her own family that she had never known, so she did not feel as betrayed as she had when she had found out about her grandmother having a sister. Thus, she considered the possibility of going to where her grandmother was to help her, but the moment she looked at her grandfather before standing up, she declined that option. Alike it had happened to her, he had not known about that cupboard either, and that had left him frozen on his seat.

Unaware of how her husband and granddaughter had reacted to her actions, Leagsaidh put the small key behind her nightgown again and took a deep breath before opening the cupboard. She had not opened that cupboard for over fifty years, although she had guarded the key as a treasure ever since she put her secrets inside. With a trembling hand, she took the notebook that was inside of it and embraced it before saying: 'I don't understand why she lied. I can't begin to understand why she changed so much'.

Eileen looked at her grandfather, and with great sorrow in her chest, for he was still not moving, she decided to break the silence: 'What's the matter, grandma?'.

'Beethoven's Sixth symphony was our favourite song. OUR, my brother Bhaltair and I, favourite song,' said Leagsaidh, raising her voice. 'She would always complain when my brother and I played it or discussed anything about classical music. And then, all of a sudden, she became interested in it? She found out her tastes weren't that far from ours? Damn it that Leon!'.

The unexpected turn of events had left Eileen speechless. She was still unable to see what her grandmother was holding so tightly, but she could tell that she was trembling. What had she kept so well hidden so that nobody could find it? She was eager to find out, but she did not feel like rushing her grandmother just then. Sooner or later, she would share it herself.

Leagsaidh remained for a few more minutes embracing the old notebook, fighting against her body response to the stress she was experiencing. And just when Eileen was about to stand up to help her back to her seat, she flipped the pages of the notebook until she found the one she wanted. Then, she read aloud:

Scotland, 8ᵗʰ February 1934.

It's the fifth day I can't go to school because of the flu. I'm feeling much better now, but I still feel weak. Dad reckons that I won't be able to go back for at least another five days, and that breaks my heart. I'm keeping up with my duties because Clarissa is bringing everything home for me, but I miss hanging out with my friends. It's extremely cold outside, but still, I miss that.

Also, I feel sorry for my brother. Because I can't go out, he's got to do the groceries on top of his other tasks. That's my duty, but we still have to eat, so somebody had to relay me for as long as I'm in bed. Nonetheless, since he's going to the market, he's managing to bring old newspapers home, so that we have something to talk about, other than my flu. And honestly, the one he brought today led to very interesting discussions.

After dinner, dad, Bhaltair, Clarissa and I sat in the living room together for us to discuss the latest news. Of course, we weren't up to date, but a few days behind, although we didn't care about that. We still had a good time.

Usually, we would take turns to read the news aloud, but because I would burst into coughs should I talk too much, I wasn't but listening. There were news about the local theatre having performances, and also of how bad the snowfalls had been up north. They also talked about politics, although Bhaltair refused to read those. He said that those are not news for women. Unfortunately, dad agrees with him, so even though Clarissa went ballistic about it, we still had to let it go. Nevertheless, that was nothing compared to how angry she got when Bhaltair and I (as long as my cough attacks allowed me to) started talking about Beethoven after he read a news about a memorial being held in his honour down south in England.

To be honest, I don't understand why she gets so angry all about it. He was a very talented musician. I think he's the only person I've ever heard that nobody has ever criticized, or at least not in front of me. But Clarissa... she just doesn't see it. She says that we better live in the present, and forget about what happened so many years before we were born. She claims that he's overrated and that whatever he did, he was boring and clearly had nothing else to do. Beyond her, he shouldn't have but worked the land hard. I swear I sometimes don't recognize her.

I'm really tired, but every time I lay down, I start coughing. I hope I do get a good night sleep tonight regardless. I can't wait for this flu to be over.

Eileen had carefully listened to her grandmother reading aloud the diary entry. And when she finished, she could not help but feel completely lost. Every time they discovered anything from either Nora or Klara Herrmann herself, it completely contradicted whatever Leagsaidh had to say. Why were there so many differences on what were supposed to be both sides of the same story? What made Klara lie? Why was it being so difficult to discover the truth?

- XVIII -

Nora kept looking alternately from the pendant on her chest to her friends, while she continued listening to the lyrics that some estrange voices were singing. She had no idea where the music was coming from, but the lyrics were very clear: their time was running out.

'MAKE IT STOP!' shouted Maia. The music was not very loud, but the fact that she kept her ears very tightly covered made her increase her voice tone so that she could hear herself.

The moment Nora heard Maia screaming, she realised that the protagonists were still there with them. She had been so used to facing challenges for as long as they had been inside the forest, that she had forgotten they were not alone anymore. Nevertheless, the horror that was tangible on Maia's face made Nora tremble. She herself wanted to get rid of the melody, but she did not know how to do it. And the more the lyrics were repeated, the more anxious she was getting.

She did not know what to do. As long as the lyrics kept repeating, she would not be able to get help, so she decided to sit down and think as clearly as she could. She knew that that would probably infuriate Maia, but she decided to push that thought outside her mind. She needed all the space she could get in her brain to think about how to manage the situation.

She first thought about getting hold of the book to see whether she might find something on it, but she declined that option as soon as she formulated it in her head. The book had been always signed by the protagonists, and that people were right beside her, covering their ears. She then thought about having a conversation with Theresa, as she had always seemed to be one step ahead of them, but she declined that idea as well. All she could get from her now was what she already had: she was the only one able to understand the lyrics.

Apparently, her pendant was acting as a sort of amulet that was protecting her from whatever the melody could do to the others, should they had not covered their ears as Maia had ordered they did. Because its protective charm had acted from the very beginning, she had not experienced anything unusual. But the fact that her friends had done as they had been told from the very beginning, and especially because of the horror she had witnessed on Maia's face, she thought of the consequences of listening to the melody without the protective charm as something very painful.

And that did not help to clarify her mind whatsoever. She kept going on and on over what could produce such dangerous consequences, which together with the demanding message from the lyrics, made her anxiety increase at a speed she had never experienced before. Not even that one time at The Shakespeare's Globe.

Shaking her head as though the physical movement of her head would help in any way, she looked down at her chest. Her pendant was producing such an intense glow that she had to blink her eyelids a couple of times before her eyes got used to the brightness. And the moment she was able to look at the pendant without her eyes hurting, a light bulb was switched on in her brain. Everything that they had been provided with had proven useful within their endeavours; she just needed to figure out how to make the most out of her pendant.

Her sphere was decorated with the same doodles of musical notes that she had gotten on her former copy of the book. But, for the time being, they looked a bit different. And it was not just the fact that light was coming through the lines, which obviously gave them a completely different dimension. They seemed to be moving at the beat. And… could that be possible? She rubbed her eyes and had a closer look.

The musical notes were originated where the sphere joined the necklace and moved to form a spiral all the way to the complete opposite end. On their way there, they seemed to dance at the beat, and just when they were about to disappear, they became letters. The transformation happened ever so quickly, that Nora almost believed she was not seeing it, rather than actually doing so. But she decided to trust her guts.

Leaving the pendant hanging freely from her neck, she took off her backpack and opened it again. She then introduced her trembling hands in the main pocket and pulled out her music notebook and a pencil. She then waited for the melody to start all over again before writing down the lyrics:

If wise enough to discover it
And brave enough to come in
You might wish to play this
From beginning to end
From end to beginning.

No mistakes are allowed
Just one time to play it aloud
So practice now
Just before the end of the countdown.

No hand must be stopped
So if you are a lot
Try dividing it a lot
Because the countdown is not on the top.

If you succeed
You will be free
But if you don't
You will never go.

So don't be a foolish
And start practising now!

And as she had guessed it would happen, the moment she transcribed the last letter, the melody stopped altogether. Smiling widely due to her successful intervention, she ripped out the sheet and shouted they could uncover their ears, for the melody was encaged on the piece of paper she was now holding in her hand.

'Nora…,' said Gabe, with a gleeful look on his eyes. He waited for her to look at him, and right when they established eye contact, he ran to her and kissed her. It was a very soft, quick kiss that caught Nora completely by surprise. In fact, after he pulled away, she could not talk, but she did feel her body talking for her. She let go of the piece of paper where she had written down the lyrics, to cover her reddened face. Despite that, she could still listen to Gabe whispering: 'I never doubted you'd do it'.

Clap, clap, clap. Maia sardonically clapped her hands whilst talking: 'she's still ages away to set us all free. Let's leave the romance for when we can see daylight again'.

'Excuse me, madam!' exclaimed Theresa in a very angry voice. Her brother kissing Nora had taken her by surprise as well, just like everyone else in the room. But that did not mean she was going to allow Maia to be that rude to any of her friends. 'I've seen your terrified face while the melody was being played, and that leads me to think you had never gained power over the melody at all, am I wrong?'.

'How dare you talk to me like that? I could bewitch you with a flip of my hand, you know…'.

'But you will not because you need us,' said Theresa, while kneeling down next to the sheet of paper Nora had ripped out from her notebook. She had not yet read the lyrics, but she had always been a step ahead of them all. 'You see, it's right here: no hand must be stopped, so if you are a lot, try dividing it a lot' she added, pointing at the verses she had just read.

Theresa had grabbed the sheet of paper very tightly while showing it to Maia, for she had expected her to prove her authority within the group by getting hold of it. But, instead of that, she had turned around so that nobody could see her face.

'She can't read, and that frightens her to death. It's the unknown that we are the most afraid of,' said Cynthia after a few silent seconds.

'If she can't read, then she can't write either...,' thought Mark aloud.

'Indeed, Mark. But that's not the point here, because Cynthia can read,' said Theresa. That latest statement had made Nora forget about her reddened grimace. How could she have figured that out? Had it been while she had been trying to find out how to make the melody stop? She wanted to ask Theresa a lot of questions, but when her friend resumed, she decided they would have time for that later on: 'have the lyrics ever been known to you?'.

'No, they have not,' said Cynthia. Alike it had happened while their communication with the protagonists had been through the book, it seemed as though they would not be sharing too much information from scratch.

'So it means you don't have full control of everything that goes around here,' said Theresa.

'No, we don't,' replied Cynthia. Nora thought she saw a smile on Cynthia's face despite the negative responses.

'But you did produce the letters on the book, as well as the footprints. Didn't you?' asked Theresa again.

'Yes, we did,' replied Cynthia. And this time, Nora was sure there had been a wider smile on Cynthia's face.

'So as much as you've been trying to make us think you know everything, you're as lost as we are. Why would you do that?'.

'First of all, we are not as lost as you are. We are a few steps ahead. Just to set it clear,' said Cynthia. Despite having sounded firm, her voice tone had been tender. 'And the reason to why we have done that... will you believe me if I say we didn't have any other option?'.

'I guess we could, but that doesn't mean we will. We might be underage, but we're not stupid. There's a reason behind everything, whether or not one is willing to tell the truth,' said Theresa. She had tried to sound as firm, yet as tender, as Cynthia had. And, beyond Nora, she had achieved that.

'Clever girl,' said Maia, turning around. 'I like you. I've liked you from the very beginning actually. But Cynthia hasn't spoken other than the truth: we had no other option. Ever since we got locked in here, we've been given the power to communicate with the outside world through the legends' book. I can't read myself, neither can Nor, but we were locked in here long before the book existed. We were the first protagonists. Andreas, Francesco and Cynthia were dragged in by their curiosity, and had not had any other option than to wait for your arrival'.

'But why us?' asked Mark. He had been following the conversation as though he had been watching a tennis match. Thus, tired of looking from one person to another, he had decided to voice his thoughts.

'My brother and I have been trying to get out of this cave for as long as I can remember. We just leveraged every opportunity we had to attract dauntless readers. But trust me, every time we tried, we didn't know what would happen. We played our cards, and it wasn't until you four came together that we knew we had found our saviours,' said Maia.

'And how did you know that?' asked Mark back.

'Because of this,' said Maia, pointing at the wall that was furthest from them.

None of the teenagers had paid any attention to the walls while in the room, so they had naturally not realised that unlike in the corridor, the wall that Maia was pointing at had a drawing on it. A drawing that contained a bigger version of the doodle at the bottom of the protagonists' warning page from the collapsed book: a cave surrounded by trees, to which a path made out of footprints was directed, and that was full of musical notes.

19

After having heard what Leagsaidh had written as a kid in her diary, Eileen and her grandfather had remained seated for a few minutes, completely unable to voice their feelings. Both of them had tried to speak several times, but every single one of those tries had died on their throats, for they had not been able to find the correct words to accurately express their thoughts.

Frustrated by the sudden and frequent change of events, Eileen decided, after a few minutes of failed attempts to express her thoughts, that she was done for the day. Without asking her grandparents, she had stood up, walked her way to where the photo albums were, and put them all inside the boxes. She had nonetheless kept with her the latest letter of Klara Herrmann that she had found. After that, she had just left the living room silently.

On her way upstairs however, she had barely lifted her feet. She had played cool in front of her grandparents, as she had considered that they had had enough emotions for the day. Her grandmother had finally opened up about things she had never talked about to anyone, and that would have been a big issue by itself. But they had gone a bit further on their rollercoaster of emotions. Some of the things they had discovered, through either the hand of Nora or Klara, had contradicted, or at least not matched completely, what Leagsaidh had had to say. And that had been very frustrating.

When she reached her room, Eileen was still feeling very frustrated. Such was the case in fact, that she slammed the door a bit more harshly than she had intended to. 'Damn it! Damn it! Damn it!' she exclaimed while knocking at the inside of her room door. She then looked at her left hand, where she had the letter from Klara Herrmann, and said aloud: 'I don't know whether I admire or loathe you. I truly don't'.

Shaking her head, she let go of the letter that glided its way to the floor and went straight to her desk. For as long as she could remember, she had had a very busy mind, and the only thing that had allowed her to put her thoughts in order had been writing. What she could not remember however was whether she had found comfort through writing because she enjoyed it, or because that was the way she was indirectly expressing herself.

As a kid, she had written short stories and had even won a few local contests. But she had produced other stories that she had never let anyone read. Not even her grandfather. And it was not because she was not proud of those, because she was very proud indeed. Her problem with them had always been the fact that they contained a huge emotional load about her inner battles. And just the thought of somebody else reading them made her feel uneasy.

As much as she would not let anyone read her private stories, they were her go-to whenever she felt overloaded with emotions. Whichever the nature of those emotions. To her, her private stories were like an X-ray photo of her soul that she could stare at whenever she needed to. And that was what her subconscious had led her to after everything that had happened.

That time however, she did not know whether her uneasiness could be ameliorated by her previous experiences. It was true that she had once had to face the fact of being put in a position where she was supposed to think of people in a way that she could not. Even though her grandparents had never forced her to love her parents, she had always felt that her grandmother had not felt as comfortable as her grandfather had about the fact that, even when she tried, she could not miss someone she had never met.

She had endless times asked about how her parents were like, what they liked and what they made for a living. As a teenager, she had even asked about how her parents had treated her. And even if she could remember that now, those had never been her memories. Or at least she had never felt them as genuine memories. It was true that she had created a story that she was becoming more and more comfortable to talk about, but that was all it was: a story.

And the problem had always been that she was not the author of that story. She had not created it and thus felt a bit like an intruder. Even though she had never felt comfortable talking about her fears, or her love struggles, or even her dreams, she had felt that writing while feeling those emotions had been very healing. Regardless of whether she journaled or came up with a new story from scratch.

She had been rewriting her former Nora story since she had arrived at Pitlochry. It had been an interesting process so far, but she just wished she had had more time for it. Although she had to agree that the emotions she was experiencing, as well as the discoveries she was making, were going to add a different dimension to her story. Despite the first version having been finished for years, she was allowing herself to be carried to wherever her heart led her to. It was true she had never met her parents, but she wanted to tribute them, for she owed them her life.

Thus, forgetting about the reason why she was feeling like she was feeling, or at least trying to do so, she opened the *Novel in progress* file on her laptop, scrolled the document down to the last paragraph she had changed, and started working on it again. She had never been someone who imposed her ways upon others, but she enjoyed the fact that she was the master of the situation. She had always imagined herself behind the scenes, doing all the workload that nobody seems to take into consideration unless things do not go as expected.

But, above all, she enjoyed the fact that she could give her characters all the skills she ever wished for herself. With all due respect for psychologists, she felt the process of writing and reading was the therapy she needed. And it was not because she was unhappy about her life, but because it allowed her to see herself from the perspective of somebody else: her future self would only be allowed to judge within the frame she had provided the character with. Nothing else, nothing less.

She set the rules, and she had to accept them. Although she would lie if she ever said she never struggled within the process. Every time she had written one of those short stories, she had had to leave aside anything that was not essential for the progression of the story. But this time, it was different. She did not have to work within an established frame. This time, the sky was the limit.

Although it did not mean it was any less difficult. Sometimes words would roll off her fingers with such an ease that she wondered why she had become a scientist, instead of a novelist. Whereas other times she would struggle with every single paragraph. Despite that however, she never exasperated. Whenever the story seemed to get written itself, she just enjoyed her capabilities; and when it did not, she just looked for her strong points, for her mantra was: anything worth having is worth fighting for.

Thus, with all the willpower she found within herself, she pushed aside from her mind anything that had to do with Klara Herrmann and the mystery around her and focused on her project. She typed, and erased, and retyped, and read and reread alone in her room for hours. An even though she struggled with concentration at the beginning, by the time she realised she had produced a good amount of work, it was already dark outside. She felt rewarded for her performance and in peace with herself. She so much needed that before facing what was to come.

Yawning heavily, she decided to end her writing for the day. She saved the file, sent the updated copy to her grandfather by email and went to brush her teeth to get ready for bed. Both when she walked out and back in her room she passed next to the letter from Klara Herrmann, but she did not seem to either see or remember it was there. That was how hard she had restrained herself from not enjoying her writing process.

- XIX -

The four teenagers stared at the drawing on the wall with their mouths widely opened. Even Theresa was surprised that the protagonists had known they were going to meet their saviours. But her amazement did not last long.

'As much as I would like to overwhelm you with thousands of questions, I think we should get focused on how to get out of here,' said Theresa, focusing her eyes on the protagonists, who were all together. 'To start with, we are on a countdown, and I would not like to wait decades to be set free because we ran out of time. The lyrics are very explicit about what we shall do. Are there any instruments in here?'.

'If there are, we haven't seen them,' said Nor. He had a very deep voice, but he sounded neither demanding nor sure of himself. If at all, his voice was mournfully tinged. That much tinged in fact, that Nora started with her daydreaming again, so that she did not succumb to desperation.

She was still feeling anxious about the whole situation. She had indeed succeeded on her first all-alone challenge, but as Maia had so very well pointed out, they were still ages away from being set free. First of all, they were supposed to play the melody before their time ran out, but neither did they know how much time they had left, nor what were they supposed to play. And second of all, their hosts were not of any help.

The letters they had gotten on the book had been clarifying, but they had not said anything beyond what they had guessed. Nora had known that for quite some time now, but she had wished for a bigger help by the time they had to face the final challenge. To her surprise however, the protagonists had turned out to be prisoners as well, which instead of answering the questions she had, did not but add a bunch of new ones. And, even though she did not want to be desperate, she was finding it more difficult than she had wished she would.

But should she stop thinking about their chances to get away, the other thing that came to her mind was the kiss that Gabe had given her. It had been such a sudden and unexpected movement on his behalf, that she had not had time to set aside a space on her mind to think about the consequences that could have. As dedicated as she had been her whole life to becoming a world-renowned pianist, she had not had that much time to think about starting her dating life. Like any other girl her age, she had had crushes on boys she had met, but she had never made that a priority in her life. Her mantra had always been: whatever is meant to happen, will indeed happen, whether it takes a month, a year, or a decade, but it will happen.

Although that did not mean she had not imagined how her first kiss would be. From what she could remember from her science lessons just then, the physical contact with others makes our brains generate substances that reduce the heartbeat to a calmer state, and thus make one feel less anxious, and less worried about anything in the environment. But she had felt quite the opposite. If she recalled the moment however, there had roughly been any physical contact between them.

After having said her name, Gabe had walked the few steps that had separated them, and had softly and quickly kissed her on her lips. She did not know which had been the reasons as to why he had reacted like that, but she wished he had not done so in front of so many people. Her body response to the kiss had been triggered from the moment their lips had come together, and minutes later she still felt the consequences.

She had felt a special connection with Gabe from the very beginning, but she had been so caught up in trying to understand why they had been involved in such a weird story, that she had not realised that he had felt the same connection. Yet the answers she needed would need to wait for some other time. She needed to get focused on figuring out how to get out of that cave.

She looked around to see whether she had let any detail pass unnoticed, and something inside of her got twisted when she realised she had spent some valuable time thinking about her own things, whereas the rest had been trying to decide what they could do next.

'We sometimes have to put our thoughts in order before we can do something with or for someone,' said Francesco. Nora turned around alarmed, for she had not heard him approaching her from behind. When he realised he had startled her, he apologized and continued talking: 'I remember when I got locked up in here as though it was yesterday. I could have left, but I came back. I've had second thoughts about it ever since then, and not even today I'm sure of whether I made the right decision. But fear lead my actions, and I'm not ashamed of recognising that'.

Nora could not understand anything of what Francesco was saying, but she considered her asking straight away would be quite rude. Unluckily for her, her unwanted ability to show her emotions in her face spoke for her, although Francesco seemed to find that amusing, for he giggled a bit before resuming:

'Do you remember the legend? The original text, I mean, not the letters'.

'Do you mean the one about Fear monster?' asked Nora back. When Francesco nodded as a reply to her question, she hurried to add: 'yes, I do. Why?'.

'Because I'm the one who *escaped* to seek help but got completely ignored. My brother and I were fleeing justice when we came across the book. At that time we did not think of the consequences that could report us. All we cared about was the fact that, by using the book, we were going to get our prosecutors to lose our track. We hadn't but robbed a few apples to feed our younger siblings, but we were accused of murdering a peasant whose body was found just a few minutes after we had taken the apples, so we had to flee.

»If it hadn't been for the instructions we got from the book, we wouldn't have lived, so I guess that was one of the reasons why I decided to go back into the forest when nobody believed me. That, and the fact that my brother had been swallowed by the cave. I can't remember how long we had walked until we got to the entrance, but when we got there, I remember I felt uneasy about the whole situation. I had the feeling that we were being observed and, even though I tried, I couldn't get my brother to reconsider our journey. We had an argument, a very agitated one, and I reckon I said things I didn't really feel, but when I turned around to apologise… everything happened ever so quickly. He introduced his pendant on the whole by the entrance and, in a matter of seconds, the rocks moved towards each other, and he was gone.

»I shouted his name until I had no voice, but he wouldn't reply. I ran towards the caves once they retook their former position, but he was nowhere to be seen. I tried to walk through one of the entrances, but every time I tried, I got repelled by an invisible force. I was hopeless, so I decided to seek help. I didn't have any other option but to risk myself to try and save my brother, so I went to the nearest settlement. I tried to talk to the least number of people as possible, as I didn't know whether our heads were under reward, but none of them believed me.

»I felt hopeless, sad, scared, alone,… and any other feeling that one could experience in a situation such as the one I lived. It took me a while to sort out what I was feeling. I wandered and thought, and thought and wandered for a long time, and the only conclusion I reached was that I wanted to be with my older brother. I couldn't go back to my family because nobody in our village would have forgotten the incident, and I knew I wouldn't be welcomed in the village by the forest either. I could have left and settled somewhere else; that would have been the easy option. But easy doesn't necessarily mean right.

»It's true I could have lived a different life, and I'd lie if I said I have never thought of what would have happened if I hadn't decided to come back. But if I hadn't made that decision, I wouldn't have met you. We wouldn't be having this conversation and I wouldn't be making an impact in your life. I trusted in you even before you got hold of your former copy of the book. So, here and now I say: cheers to all the bad decisions we made that led us to meet great people,' said Francesco, raising his hand as though he had a glass on it. He then mimicked a group cling and, while he was pretending to take a sip, he winked an eye at Nora.

Nora felt her face redden at the sweet words that Francesco had dedicated her, so she looked away. Without asking, he had shared his story with her, and that had made her think about how we all think that our problems are always the biggest and the worst. Even though that she was locked up in a cave, which was disturbing enough, the other things that had busied her mind had not been close to what Francesco had experienced. He had been, together with his brother, accused of a murder he had not committed, which had obliged them to leave everything and everyone behind. And she could not help but feel sorry for them.

But why was everyone so convinced of her capabilities? Francesco, as well as Gabe, and the thought of that made her smile ever so quickly, had pointed out that she was going to be the one to set them free. Unlike her, they had no doubts on that matter, although she could begin to understand why Francesco could feel that way. He had been locked up for centuries, and the only hope to being set free again had been that they found the dauntless readers that matched the characteristics that were drawn on the wall of the room they were in. Nonetheless, he had said that he had believed in her even before she had been assigned a scrawl. Could it be that he had solely said that so that she believed in herself? Was he playing that trick on her, so she could set them free?

Feeling bad for having thought bad of Francesco after he had dedicated such nice words to her, she silently reprimanded herself and looked away yet another time. Because she had been looking away twice in a row, she had been left with no other possibility than staring at the drawing on the wall. It looked magnificent, and despite having been done over rock, all the details were neat and precise. And the more she looked at it, the more she thought of why she had been chosen. Her friends had pointed out that she had been chosen the leader for the qualities she had within herself, but she doubted that had been it. There had to be more. To start with, their grandmothers had been linked to the legend as well, or so she thought.

She kept on staring at the drawing for a few more minutes until she noticed something that she had not seen before. Frowning, she looked around to see what the others were doing, and when she confirmed that nobody was paying any attention to her, she stood up and walked to the wall. The four scrawls from her friends and herself were the most vivid, but they were not the only ones. Some fainter lines formed yet new scrawls. She identified five new scrawls and that made her smile. Turning around she asked:

'Correct me if I'm wrong, but are your pendants decorated with either a squirrel, a bird, a stag, a wolf, or a flower?'.

'How did you figure that out?' asked Maia, obviously scared of the fact that she had found that out without asking.

'In the same place that you found reassurance of us being your saviours,' said Nora, pointing at the drawing on the wall.

Theresa smiled widely at her friend and then asked: 'What do you reckon all our scrawls being on the same drawing mean?'.

'Well, I don't know whether when Maia said it she was fully aware of it, or she was just lucky, but our pendants were indeed our way in and will also be our way out. I haven't seen the cavities until I came closer because they are not as pronounced as the ones outside, but they are here. We have to introduce our pendants in them to get past this wall. I don't reckon we'll see daylight straight away, but I'm confident about this step'.

When she finished talking, the others came closer to the drawing and observed it in search of the cavities. Laughs, emotional tears and hugs started happening at the moment each of them realised that they were walking in the right direction. And, as one, they removed the necklaces from their necks and set them free.

The pendants flew their respective ways and, once they were all aligned, they got inserted into the cavities by an invisible force. None of them was surprised when a very bright light was produced, and thus nobody had fear expressed on their faces. They were feeling the taste of freedom again, and that can knock down any bad feeling.

20

Despite not having set an alarm before falling asleep the previous night, Eileen woke up early the following morning. She had fallen asleep with the curtains up, and thus daylight had invaded the room as soon as the trees had let it pass through their branches. She had had such a nice night sleep however, that she did not feel tired at all.

She blinked her eyes a couple of times for her pupils to get used to the amount of daylight before getting up. Then, she stood up and opened the window. Putting her hands over the windowsill, she let the morning breeze welcome her to a new day.

The letter from Klara Herrmann was still lying on the floor by her room door. She had taken it with her instinctively, without a clear mindset of what she could do with it. She had already read it, and even though there did not seem to be any hidden information on it, she had taken it with her anyway. She had knowingly ignored it, as she felt she needed to focus on something else so that by the time she went back to it, she could come up with fresh ideas.

She turned around to let her body rest on the windowsill and looked at the letter. She had mixed feelings about her great aunt. She was curious about her story and the reasons she had had to leave everything behind, but the fact that she had not seemed to be honest with the people she loved really pulled her back.

Yet she knew that the only way her mind would let the matter at bay would be by getting to the very end of it. Although the more she thought of what they could do next, the least number of ideas of things they had not done already popped in her head. The finding of the captions her mother had made for every single photo had been a great discovery by itself, but because they only had the letters that Nora had received, they could not but guess what she might have known.

Thus, if they genuinely wanted to find out the truth, the only option they had left was contacting Klara Herrmann herself. Their one and only problem was however, that they did not know how to do that. The letters had not been kept inside their shipping envelopes, so they did not have her address. And the fact that they were sure she had lived in different countries, did not but widen the searching area.

Feeling frustrated and in need of a talk with her grandfather, she grabbed some clean clothes and headed to the bathroom to get a much-needed shower. Before voicing her thoughts, she first had to put them in order. Once done, she went downstairs to have breakfast.

When she entered the kitchen, she found her grandmother silently eating some eggs with bacon. She had endless times told her that she should not have such greasy breakfasts unless she was going to exercise afterwards, but she decided that day was not a good day for an argument.

'Morning, grandma. How do you do today?' Eileen greeted her grandmother while opening the fridge to get hold of some milk.

'Good, honey, good,' said Leagsaidh. 'Although I'm a bit ti'ed. Yer grandpa and I stayed up until late'.

'How come?' said Eileen, surprised by the confession.

'We just talked 'bout eve'ything we've discovered 'bout Clarissa. After all these years, I neve' thought I'd talk 'bout her again. And...,' Leagsaidh's voice cracked at that point. Eileen knew that that meant she was going to say something that would make her emotional, so she decided to wait for her to be ready to continue: 'I apologised again to him fer having kept all that information 'bout my past. He wasn't worth the half-truths I told him. Bette' late than neve', ye know'.

'Indeed, grandma, indeed,' said Eileen, putting her hand over her grandmother's to comfort her. Using her other hand to take the last sip she had left on her mug, she asked: 'and where is grandpa now? I'd like to talk to him'.

'He's in the backya'd, taking care of the vegetable ga'den. We might have veggie soup fer lunch today'.

'Oh, I'd love to! It's been a while since I last had some. I'll go talk to grandpa now, and then I'll come back and help you,' said Eileen. She then cleaned up the portion of the breakfast table she had used and, before leaving the kitchen, she kissed her grandmother on her forehead.

As Eileen had grown up, she had found their backyard smaller and smaller. But she knew it was a matter of perspective. She had inherited her height from her father's side and thus was taller than the average. She had not found that disturbing whatsoever, although she had felt observed and pointed at while growing up.

The trampoline that had occupied most of the backyard had been gone for years, and it had been replaced by a vegetable garden that seemed to get bigger and bigger every year. As for her old treehouse, which had never been over the tree branches, but right beneath them, had been turned into her grandfather's storage room.

'Mo'ning, honey,' said Alick, waving his left hand. He then walked a few steps to where the water tap was, to fill the watering can he had carried in his right hand. When everything was set, he resumed: 'I read the update this mo'ning. The sto'y is getting bette' and bette'. I've got a few favourite pa'ts already, but I feel that the best is yet to come. What a turn of events though. If it weren't because the characters have got the same names as in yer former story, I wouldn't say it's the same one. I'm honoured I'm the first one to read it'.

'Ooh, thanks, grandpa. Despite not having written for a looong time,' she said, really emphasizing the o on long, 'when I started this project I felt everything I felt when I wrote as a kid. I allowed myself to see life through the eyes of my inner kid. I think it's mental healing to do that from time to time. But…'.

'But ye didn't come to talk 'bout yer story,' said Alick. While Eileen had been talking, he had closed the water tap and carried the watering can to the vegetable garden to start watering the plants. But as his grandchild had tried to change topics, he had stopped. 'Lemme finish here and we'll talk afte'wards'. Then, he continued watering the plants.

Eileen turned around and walked towards the bench her grandfather had handcrafted for her when she was ten. It was made of wood and contained silhouettes of her favourite rugby players, although the sun, and especially the rain, had erased most of the details he had so carefully added. Before sitting down, she took from her back pocket the letter from Klara Herrmann and started reading it again.

'I can't read German, but I don't think the'e a'e any hidden messages on it,' said Alick, sitting down right next to Eileen.

'Grandma told me you were up until late last night. She said she apologised once again for having kept so many secrets from you. And this is all my fault,' said Eileen, raising her eyes to look at her grandfather. She did not express but sadness on her face. 'If I hadn't broken that frame, nothing of this would have happened. We're on a dead-end street now. I haven't but stir the hive… for nothing!'.

'Don't whip yerself! Truth always finds its way to the surface. Besides, I'm not angry at yer grandma. All those things happened before we met. And even though it was her story, I never forced her to tell me anything she didn't feel comfortable talking 'bout. I've trusted her frem day one, and that was the reason she ended up opening 'bout it. She could have chosen to remain silent, to say nothing at all, but she sha'ed her story with us instead. Rega'dless of how much we think we know someone, neithe' we're in their head to see life as they do, nor we unde'stand how much their insecurities can draw them back.

»Nonetheless, I do unde'stand ye want to get to the end. It's comprehensible; and if I'm honest with you, I do as well. I'm also curious 'bout the reasons Clarissa had to do what she did, but I wouldn't let any of this hu't my wife. She's gone through enough already.' Alick had made those last confessions looking at the kitchen window, from where he could see his wife.

Eileen looked first at her grandfather, and then at her grandmother through the kitchen window. She had always known that Alick would support her on anything she did, but she comprehended the fear that exposing his wife caused him. She did not want to do any wrong moves, but her problem then was that she could not do any move at all.

Feeling lost, she found herself looking at the letter again. She reread it for the sixth time since she had found it, and just when she was about to refold it to let it go, she sensed the relief that is left on a piece of paper when one handwrites on it. It would not have caught her attention should it had not been over a white area. She passed her fingers over it again on both sides and then took the paper closer to her eyes. Jumping from the bench, she rushed indoors. She was so focused on her latest discovery that she did not hear her grandfather shouting at her what was it that she had found.

She did not stop running until she got to her room. Once there, she opened all the drawers on her desk until she found a pencil and then used it to paint over the area on relief. She was not surprised when a phone number, with a dialling code corresponding to Germany, was shown. Not thinking about the bill that she would get for an international call, she dialled it.

Her heartbeat raised with every tone she heard, although it was nothing compared to when they ended because the call had been answered.

'Frau Herrmann hier. Hallo?' said a feminine voice on the other end of the line.

'Haa...hallo. Ist es Klara Herrmann?' said Eileen. She was shaking so badly.

'Ja, genau. Das bin ich. Wer ist da?' said a very contradicted Klara.

'Ich bin die Tochter von Nora und Aksel,' said Eileen. 'Aber dafür rufe ich dich nicht an. Ich rufe an, weil meine Großmutter deine Schwester ist. Sie heißt Leagsaidh'.

Eileen heard the noise that Klara Herrmann's phone made when it hit the ground. She also heard how she started crying.

- XX -

When Nora felt the necklace hanging from her neck again, she knew that the wall that had contained the drawing was gone. There had not been a single noise that had indicated that any movement had occurred, but she felt confident that by the time she opened her eyes, the scenery would have changed.

She blinked her eyes a couple of times before her pupils got used to the amount of light and allowed her to keep her eyes open without them hurting. It took them a few extra seconds to allow any image to be formed in her brain. And, when she saw what had been kept hidden behind the wall, she could not help but nervously giggle at the sight of it.

Still rock-walled, the new room that laid in front of them was double the size of the room they were standing at, and was empty except for whatever it was that was right in the middle. Nora tried to silently guess what that could be by simply staring at it, whilst her companions talked.

'Are we going to jump from one room to another for eternity?' exclaimed Mark. 'The only corridor that this room has is back to where we've already been, and there are no paintings to suggest there is a hidden door anywhere…'.

'It's the first time we ever see this part of the cave. I can't tell how big it is, but I'm starting to think we haven't seen but the very entrance,' said Nor. Pointing at the object covered by the black blanket that laid right in the middle of the room, he added: 'Although that can't be coincidental. Do you reckon it's safe to uncover it?'.

'I hope it is safe because I'm going to uncover it right now,' said Andreas, walking straight to the object. Except for when the protagonists had greeted the teenagers, Andreas had not spoken a single word, and so it took Nora completely by surprise that he was suddenly so willing to take action.

And, just by the time he was about to pull the blanket away, Maia shouted: 'DON'T DO IT! You can very well get us all killed'.

'I rather risk it, to be honest. I'm fed up with being locked up in this cave. I have lost track of how much time I've spent in here, only able to wander within a mile from this cave. Don't you want to get to the end? Don't you want to be free again?' asked Andreas back.

'Of course, I do! But not at whatever cost' said Maia. For once, Nora perceived concern in her speech. 'I don't think a couple of hours would make any difference compared to the centuries we've already been here for. I rather do things right for once'.

Nora wondered what had happened to Maia for her to say that, but decided to push away those thoughts to concentrate on the big issue they were facing. She was not surprised they had been led to a different room instead of outside the cave. At the end of the day, they had not yet fulfilled the task they had been imposed through the lyrics. But the fact that there was not a way to find out how much time they had left did not but alter her relaxed status.

As determined as Andreas had seemed to uncover the object, he had forfeited his attempts the moment Maia had shouted at him. Nora had heard more imposing tones from her, but the truth was that she had only spent with her a couple of hours, yet had to agree that Maia was intimidating. Thus, thinking of what best to do next, she sought Theresa for help.

'Do you reckon we have many more rooms to get passed?' whispered Nora on Theresa's ear.

'I don't think so, no,' said Theresa back. 'And... to be honest, I think we shall uncover that,' she added, pointing at the middle of the room. 'You know I'm more of a think-things-through-first-before-taking-action type of person, but our time is running out. I don't know how much we were given, but it took us a while to get here. And the more we hesitate now, the less time we'll have afterwards. Yet we have to convince Ma...'.

'Or we could do it without asking for permission,' interrupted Gabe. He glanced at Nora ever so quickly, to then hold his sister's hands on his before adding: 'Sis, they know as much as we do now. If it weren't for us, they wouldn't be here at all'.

'Neither will we,' pointed Theresa out.

'Indeed. But should the time run out, we'll be locked in here forever. There are no paintings suggesting any future saviours. It's now or never.' Gabe let go of his sister's hand and, without letting his intentions be noticed until it was too late to mend it, he walked all the way to the middle of the room and pulled the black blanket away.

Maia, Nor and Mark shouted and then covered themselves as though they expected things to blow away. Andreas was startled at the sudden movement of the blanket whilst his brother alternately looked from Gabe to Theresa and Nora, who had been petrified. Unlike the others, they had known what Gabe was going to do, but they held their breathe until the object was completely uncovered. And when it was, their breath did not come back straight away. Not in a hundred years Nora had thought that she would get scared at the sight of a piano.

The moment her eyes recognized the object, something inside of her got twisted. Her eyesight got tunnel-like, and her ears started buzzing. Not even today does she know how much time she spent like that, but she does get uneasy whenever the thought comes back to her mind. What made her so nervous however was not the fact that the instrument they had to play to be set free was a piano. She even found that coherent, somehow. What made her the most afraid was the sand clock that was right on top of it. She knew that the sand had been falling for a while, but she did not expect their remaining time to be that little.

'No mistakes are allowed. No hand must be stopped. No mistakes are allowed. No hand must be stopped,' she mumbled to herself, with her eyes still focused on the sand clock. She had listened to the lyrics enough times for them to have been carved onto her brains. And, in such a nervous condition, the verses that made her the most scared were the first ones that came to her mind.

'LOOK WHAT YOU'VE DONE! YOU'VE GOT HER CURSED!' shouted Maia at Gabe when she regained her will.

'For goodness sake!' exclaimed Gabe. 'She's not cursed. She's just afraid. What would have you done instead?'.

'I would have…I would have…'.

'Let me help you,' said Theresa, all of a sudden. Given their current circumstances, she sounded insultingly calmed. 'The fact that you took a bad decision once, does not mean that every decision you make will be a disaster. It's okay to make mistakes, as well as it is okay to be lucky' she added, glancing at her brother. Gabe blushed, but Theresa did not see it, for she had turned to look at Maia again. 'I understand that you regret whatever you did that brought you here, but you have to let it go of you. Our past indeed makes the essence of what we are, yet we can't let it define our present. We shouldn't be but whatever we choose to be. And I know you want to be free. We will get out of this cave, and we will do that together'.

Theresa offered her hand to Maia and, to her surprise, the rest joined her. Even Nora, who had been brought back from her dreaming state. None of them noticed anything unusual happening the moment all their hands got into contact, but the truth was that the moment they all committed to the task, the sand clock grew a few inches.

'Guys, trust me when I say I don't want to break apart this magical moment, but that piano ain't getting played by itself,' said Mark, pointing his thumb backwards, towards where the piano was. He made everyone laugh, which helped alleviate the tension in their muscles.

'Right. You're very right, Mark,' said Nora, rubbing her head nervously. She knew that the others were expecting her to lead their way, and thus was trying to find the best way to command her orders. 'You know what the lyrics say: we all have to play the melody. I can get the partiture written down and divided for nine people. It shouldn't take me more than half an hour, at the most. Mark,' she said, focusing on him, 'since you can play the piano as well, please, grab a few sheets of paper from my notebook, and explain them the basics. Then, draw a piano keyboard. You and I will be playing the more difficult parts, but they have to take part as well,' she said, pointing her fingers at the others. She then added: 'as for you all… don't panic. We'll handle the situation'.

Nora dedicated a reassuring smile at them all, leaving Gabe for last on purpose. She wished for him to understand everything that she wanted to say, and then turned around to go back to her backpack. She flipped the pages until she got to the empty ones and then pulled up a few. She handed most of them to Mark and kept one for her to write the partiture. She had once played The Sixth Symphony by Beethoven, so she felt confident about the transcription process. She felt uneasy about the others having to play the piano as well, but she decided to push that thought away. Negativity was not going to take her anywhere good.

As she had predicted, about half an hour later she was done, and thus they could start practising. While she had been filling the pentagrams, she had listened to how Mark had explained everything to the others. And she had to agree that he felt natural doing that. He had been bombarded with questions, and not a single time had he raised his voice. He was meant for that. As well as she was meant to lead their whereabouts.

She silently joined the semicircle Theresa, Gabe, Maia, Nora, Andreas, Francesco and Cynthia had formed around Mark and waited for him to finish his explanation. She then handed the partiture to him.

None of them realised that the moment Mark got hold of the sheet of paper that contained the partiture, the sand clock started running again. It had been stopped for as long as they had been getting ready for the practising time. Despite having been locked up in a cave, luck was on their side.

21

Eileen waited with the phone in her ear for minutes. She had decided to address whoever picked the phone in German and thus have the surprise factor on her side. That way, she had been able to at least confirm that she had gotten the shreds of evidence right.

Although faint, she could hear Klara Herrmann crying and blowing her nose the whole time. She could also hear how she spoke to someone, but because the mobile phone was away from them, she could not understand what they were saying. She could tell whoever had spoken had been a woman, and she did not have to wait long until she found out to whom the voice belonged.

'Hallo? Wer ist da?' said the unknown feminine voice at the other end of the line. Eileen felt her whole body shake. The hand she was holding her mobile phone with felt all sweaty, and her voice would not come out. 'Wer ist da?' repeated the unknown voice again.

'Haa...hallo. Ich heiße Eileen. Ich muss mit Klara Herrmann jetzt sprechen. Können Sie ihr bitte das Telefon geben?'.

'Entschuldigen Sie, aber meine Mama kannst du jetzt nicht sprechen. Warum rufst du an?' said Sandra Herrmann. Eileen did not need her to say her name, as she already knew that Klara had only had a daughter.

'Sandra...'.

'Warte! Woher kennst du meinem Namen?' said Sandra, clearly nervous by the fact that she had been addressed by her name.

'Sandra ich… wir kennen uns nicht. Naja, ich denke schon. Ich bin die Tochter von Nora und Aksel. Ich muss wirklich mit deiner Mama sprechen. Bitte'. Although she could not see Sandra, Eileen knew that the mention of her parents had made Sandra shiver. Out of all people that could have phoned her mother, anyone related to the long-time gone young couple was the latest she expected.

'Warum musst du mit ihr sprechen?'. She was going to be a rough interlocutor, but as much as Eileen wanted to put pressure on her, she needed to be careful. Otherwise, the phone call could be hung up.

'Ich habe einige Fragen, die nur sie beantworten kann. Sie und meine Mama…naja, sie haben eine gemeinsame Vergangenheit. Und… ich glaube du weißt das kann ich nicht meine Mama fragen. Bitte, gib ihr das Telefon'.

Just when she finished pleading, her bedroom door suddenly opened and both her grandparents appeared under the frame. They both carried concerned looks. Eileen had no doubt that her grandfather had mentioned how suddenly she had left when she had found out something in the letter. She was also sure that they had eavesdropped on her speaking German.

She looked at them half apologetically, half excited about her latest discovery. At the end of the day, she had been able to contact the person they had been so eagerly looking forward to contacting. She knew that she would have a lot to explain herself, but she did not have much time to give those ideas a thought, for she heard noises at the other end of the line.

'Eileen? Bist du da?' asked Klara Herrmann.

'Ja,' said Eileen.

'Und meine Schwester, ist sie mit dir?'.

'Ja,' said Eileen again.

'Gut,' said Klara, although she had not sounded happy at all. 'Und macht es dir etwas aus, den Lautsprecher aufzudrehen?'.

Eileen looked at her grandparents with a glimpse of a smile on her face. She then covered the microphone on her mobile phone before saying: 'I think you have already guessed who I'm talking to. She's asked me to put the call on speaker. Are you okay with that?'. She witnessed how her granddad caressed Leagsaidh hand and did not move until she nodded her head yes. Eileen nodded her head yes back, and then uncovered the microphone, clicked on the speaker icon and said: 'Klara, you are on speaker now. I hope you understand the need to switch to English now. Both my grandparents are here with me, and none of them speaks German'. Eileen thought about how best to address the situation, and after a few seconds pondering what to say, and how to say it, she continued talking: 'Ahmm... we've been trying to reach you for a few days now. To be honest, I didn't think we'd achieve it that fast. Anyway, regardless of how many questions we might have for you, I'd appreciate it if you could give us a heads-up. I don't think you need me explaining why we're calling, do you?'.

'No, I don't,' said Klara. 'I... I... I don't know whether you'd believe me Leagsaidh, but I'm really sorry for what I did to you. I'd understand if you want to hang up the call at any point. Nonetheless, I hope you do listen to what I've got to say. It might neither be what you want to hear, nor what I want to tell you, but I'll stay loyal to the truth.

»I guess everything goes back to when you and I were kids. We weren't born in the best era for women. Our father was a very traditional man, and sadly he instilled that onto our brother as well. I felt oppressed from a very young age, and even though I had you to vent, I needed more. We had a special connection, but I loathed it when you agreed with Bhaltair on some things. We had a signed agreement on what we would do, but deep down I felt you would never leave home and disappoint Father. I guess you were the responsible of the lot.

»I, therefore, started feeling like an intruder. I don't know where the anger came from, or when I started feeling like that, but the truth is I did. And I know I was rude to you for no reason. I also know I never said that, but I couldn't handle myself. And whilst in that rollercoaster of emotions, it was when I met Leon. He was so different to Father and Bhaltair, that I fell in love with him from the very beginning. He had fled the ridiculous tradition that was raising in his country. He felt really proud of the compatriots that did not agree with the government. Beyond him, they were the truly brave part of the nation. And even though he had intense feelings about the situation, and that he would not hide his position on the matter, they were so pure, that he instilled them in me.

»It's true that we left without saying anything, but unlike you might think, the idea did not come from him, but from me. I guess you could say we dated for about a year in Scotland; although nobody noticed I was seeing someone until a few weeks before we left. By then I was so careless about what anybody thought, that I could say I allowed people to find out on purpose.

»Leon taught me German, and history of Germany, and so many other things that Father would have never allowed to be mentioned at home. I felt free with him. He truly cared about my opinion, and that, together with the sweet flavour of rebellion, was too tasty for me.

»We first moved to the Austrian border with Germany. We knew that the war could not last forever, and our hope was to one day move back to his hometown. And eventually, we did. And during that time... I'm not proud about it, but I kept myself so busy that I did not dedicate you, or Father, or Bhaltair, any thought. You represented something I wanted to get rid of so badly, that the sole thought of it made me angry. It was true I had had to leave everything behind, but that was the only way I found to be free. I quit using my English name once and for all; I would get very angry at the sole mention of it. And, as my latest rebellious act, I refused to speak my mother tongue.

»We lived in Germany for a very long time. My three kids were born there, and it's where I feel at home. We then had to relocate to Austria due to Leon's job. It took me a while to find a job, and I had been teaching at the local school for a few months only when Aksel started school. He was a very naughty little boy, so I had frequent meetings with his mother. She was there so often, that we ended up striking up a friendship. And so did our kids.

»Years passed, and our kids grew their separate ways. But the families still remained very close. My husband was a very good civil engineer, and so he advised Aksel on what subjects to take. He also suggested he did a year abroad in Germany. Little did we know then that he would find the love of his life there. Nor that she would be related to me.

»The first time Aksel brought Nora to his parents, I was shocked by how much she looked like me when I was young. And albeit neither did I point that out, nor did Leon ever mention the resemblance, I was certainly suspicious. Sometimes coincidences do happen. Nonetheless, when we started talking, she cleared out any doubts I had. Thus yes, I knew Nora my was niece, but I never told her. I had no right to do that. I had refused to that right when I left without saying goodbye. And as much as I wanted to be close to her, to be a part of her life, I couldn't decide on what she knew. I just had to settle for the fact that she had appeared in my life.

»When we got the invitation to their wedding, I cried for weeks. I knew it meant a lot to both Nora and Aksel that Leon and I made it, but we couldn't. I couldn't do that to you, Leagsaidh. I felt sorry, and miserable and everything I should have felt when I left Scotland. Reality hit me on the face, and

I couldn't but accept it. I had never apologised to you, and it would have been really mean from my side to do so right before the wedding, so that we could attend it. So yes, if I'm honest with you, I think that was the first time in my lifetime that I felt ashamed of my actions.

»Nora and I maintained contact through letters, and that was how I knew that you were doing okay. You might not believe it, but that filled me with joy. I dreamed of having this conversation with you, but I thought it was very unlikely to happen. I had forced myself away from you, so I was getting what I deserved'.

Eileen, Alick and Leagsaidh had attentively listened to everything that Klara had said. She had warned them beforehand that she was going to say things that none would like to hear, but Eileen did not think that she was going to be that open about everything.

'Klara, I appreciate your collaboration, and I thank you for that. I don't know you, but I think that you've loosened the burden you imposed on yourself. I'm sure you'll soon feel relieved,' said Eileen after a few seconds. She let go of all the air she had in her lungs and filled them again before resuming: 'I guess you might be wondering how I got hold of your phone number. Am I right?'.

'That's intriguing for sure, yes,' said Klara, sounding a lot more relieved than when she had first started talking.

'So... I came on holiday to my grandparents. Since I grew up with them, my bedroom is at their place. Long story short, a frame that contains a photo of my parents and me that I had had hanging on the wall broke, and I found a small letter from you. That led to my grandma telling both my grandpa and me about you and how you left. Neither he nor I had heard a single word about you before, so the three of us agreed to do some investigations. We searched through my parents' stuff, and one discovery led to the next one, and that one to another one, and so on until I phoned you'.

'Fair enough,' said Klara. Eileen wondered what her facial reaction had been when she had mentioned her part of the story, but she did not have much time to give that idea a thought, for Klara decided to continue talking: 'I...Leagsaidh?'.

'Ye...yes?' was all Leagsaidh could say. She had waited so many years to talk to her sister, that now that the moment had arrived she did not know how to react.

'The fact I suggested Nora she walked the aisle to The Sixth Symphony by Beethoven, was because it was your favourite song. It's true I started listening to classical music because of Leon, but the fact that song was so special to me was not because he introduced me to that kind of music, but because it reminded me of you. I thought it was the best way Bhaltair, you and I accompanied your daughter in such a special moment. I don't know whether I did the right thing, but I owed it to y...'.

'Ye owed me nothing,' said Leagsaidh, interrupting her sister. She did not sound angry, or at least not as angry as one would be in her situation. But she did sound very firm. 'Ye ought to have been he'e with me when the war took frem me the ones I loved the most. I was left alone. I felt devastated and miserable. It took me yea's to trust people again. I appreciate ye neve' told Nora who ye truly were, but that's it. I hope ye understand I can't make as though nothing happened. The fact my daughte' walked the aisle to my favourite song was fer sure emotional, but I refuse to thank ye fer that. I just can't trust ye'.

And then, silence. Leagsaidh had focused her eyesight on Eileen's mobile phone, which laid screen-up on the bed. She had not blinked whilst she had talked, but the moment she finished, she completely broke. She turned sideways towards her husband and hid her head on his chest. She started crying ever so loudly, that Klara had to address them a few times before they noticed she was speaking again.

'I know this won't change anything now, but I want to let you know that even though I've said I refused to think of any of you when I first left Scotland, that changed years after. I did learn of the passing of Bhaltair and Father, and that left me devastated. I'm not really sure how Leon found out, but when he told me, something inside of me changed. I got determined to change the anger I had inside of me into faithfulness, and that's why I named my kids after you three'.

'What do you mean? Aren't your kids named Matthias, Lukas and Sandra?' said a very contradicted Eileen.

'They are indeed. But they've all got a middle name' said Klara, containing a sob. 'Leon and I agreed to name them Matthias Duncan, Lukas Bhaltair and Sandra Leagsaidh'.

Nora and her friends, together with the protagonists, practised and practiced on the keyboard made out of paper. In the beginning, it was very difficult for them to coordinate how they had to move. They had to come up with a sort of choreography so the melody would not have unnecessary stops. That led to a few discussions that threatened the viability of their mission, but their resilient selves came out when they needed them the most.

None of them expressed their feelings aloud, yet their faces talked for them. Their concerned and focused looks suggested that no matter how afraid they were, their willingness to be set free again was a much stronger feeling.

'Do you reckon we are good to go now?' asked Mark, looking from the sand clock on top of the piano to Nora.

'I just hope we are. We don't have much time to go,' said Nora, embracing her legs. Both Mark and her had stepped back for the others to practice their parts. They needed for them to be as calm as possible, otherwise, their mission might fail altogether. 'Although, to be honest… doesn't it seem to you as though the sand falls slower and slower?'.

'Maybe it's just a trick so that we become confident and relax,' said Mark, sounding much more sure of himself than he had ever sounded. 'I wouldn't bother about it just now though. We only have one time to play the melody aloud and, from now on, the risk is the same whenever we play it'.

'Do you really think so?' asked Nora. A serious and thoughtful Mark was something she had not seen before, but she liked it.

'I do indeed,' said Mark, giggling at the face Nora had made. Again, she had not realised that her body had spoken for her, but instead of reacting defensively, he had extracted the good of it: he had impressed the leader at last! 'It's true that should we had tried to play the melody straight away, we would have failed resoundingly. But the same shall happen if we consume our time completely. What I'm trying to say is that we all reach a point when we can't improve anymore, or at least not in such a small period of time. The process of learning always works through the same pattern.

»At first, we are all excited about it. We are curious, and amazed, and impressed, and... well, you name it really. It's getting away from our comfort zone that triggers the machine. But as humans, we are limited to what we can learn. And it can be due to various reasons. We might become overwhelmed with the information cascade, we might lose curiosity because it turns out to be not what we envisioned, or we might just find something else that is suddenly more interesting to us.

»Long story short then, the excitement they started listening to me with, they will soon lose it. All they are thinking now is how best they can do their task. But the more time passes, the more confident they become, and thus the less they think of what they are actually doing, and the more they will start thinking of the fearful *what ifs*.

»So answering your question, yes, I think we've already reached the point when they start losing their concentration, and thus the risk can't but arise from now on'.

Nora had carefully listened to Mark while looking at the group that was by the paper-made piano keyboard. And as much as she wanted to refuse the idea of them having already reached their minimum risk position, she could not find any argument to defend her position. Mark had linked the thoughts so well, that there was not any crack that suggested his theory was wrong. Once they had agreed on who was going to play what and they had managed to truly memorise the movements, the practising had gone smoothly. But as

Mark had so well suggested, their concentration was starting to fade.

Nora looked at Mark for reassurance, and the look she got back really encouraged her to tackle her duty. It was true she had never asked to be put in that position, but she had to agree that she felt natural being the leader.

'Guys!' shouted Nora while standing up. 'Guys, listen! Mark and I think we are good to go. We don't have much time left anyway, so we rather do it right now'. The moment she had decided to address them, she knew that they would get nervous at the sudden change of events. They knew the moment of truth would end up arriving at some point, but the mention of it made them doubt their capabilities. But as Nora had foreseen that, she had a little speech for them: 'I know this is scary. You are to face a big challenge, on which your freedom depends. But I trust you, just like you have trusted me for this whole journey. Because whether or not I have made it patent to you, I have also doubted my capabilities. Yet it's facing the unknown that makes us grow anyway. We'll come out of this wiser and stronger. Trust me: we will.

»So now..., ready as we are, shall we begin the show?' added Nora while stepping ahead towards the piano.

While playing a stronger version of herself, Nora looked into the eyes of each one of her companions, until she reached the piano. She tried to send as much courage and calmness into them as she could and hoped that she would not need to reassure any of them. Shall any of them get seriously nervous, it could hamper their whole mission.

As a good teacher, Mark guided Maia, Nor, Andreas, Francesco, Cynthia, Theresa and Gabe to the piano. He patted them all softly on their backs and dedicated encouraging words to each of them. Of them all, he was the one who knew best how relying on friends during the hardest times can be the impulse one needs to get the best out of them. And just then, it was the time for them all to play their best selves.

Once they reunited around the piano, they dedicated a few seconds to breathe air in and out of their lungs for their heart rates to decrease, and then placed themselves in their starting positions. They practised the choreography one extra time in front of the actual piano, before betting all for one.

'I'll start in three,… two,… one,…NOW!' said Nora.

Nora played the first chords and then ceded command to Mark. Not a single time was it mentioned in the lyrics that they all had to play an equal part of the melody, so they had all agreed that Nora and Mark would not only play the most difficult parts but that they would also play the most number of chords. Thus, the moment of truth arrived when one of the others had to take action. Gabe broke the ice for them all. He was clearly very nervous, but despite his shaky hands, he managed to play his part smoothly. After that, he continued with the choreography and moved aside for his sister to play her part. She was as shaky as her brother, if not more, but she also managed to play her part without making a single mistake.

Every time a new person took action, the tension in the room seemed to increase. Yet they were so concentrated on their duty that they did not notice it until they were done. Because, as much as they loathed the moment, it passed by much faster than they imagined it would ever do. Such was the case in fact, that when Nora finished playing the last chords of the reverse composition, they all remained silent and expectant. They all wanted to be happy about their performance, yet nothing seemed to have changed. Everything looked the same. They were still locked.

'But… wasn't we supposed to…?' said Nor. He looked around, understanding nothing of what was happening.

'Didn't the lyrics say…?' said Gabe, looking as lost as Nor.

'Have you tricked us?' interrupted a very angry Maia.

'Excuse me!' exclaimed Nora. 'Why would I do that?'.

'To impress this little man here, for instance,' said Maia, grabbing Gabe by his elbow. 'There is clearly something going on between…'.

But she could not finish her sentence, for a huge crack appeared on one of the walls. It made a tremendous noise, that forced them all to cover their ears. The crack grew bigger and bigger at their sight and got accompanied by loads of other cracks. It looked as though the cave would collapse, but wherever they looked, nowhere seemed like a safe place to hide. They were trapped for good.

Further from letting the circumstances drive the situation, Nora gathered all the will she had left and walked all the way to where Gabe was. And for once, she did not think of the consequences of what she was about to do. She just felt the need to do it.

'Gabe!' shouted Nora while patting him on his back. He was startled at the sudden touch, but when he saw it was her, he could not help but smile. Despite the situation, the sole sight of her created a whole new world in front of him. A world where nothing could hurt him. 'I… I know this ain't the best moment, but I owe you something back. I… well, this is complicated… you know. But the thing is… I…'. Yet she could not finish her sentence, for Gabe had planted a kiss on her lips, again.

A kiss that, this time, Nora replied to. Because as much as she had loathed it her entire life, that time she was very pleased that her body was expressing the feeling cascade she was experiencing deep inside.

They stood in the middle of the room kissing each other, as though time had stopped right then and there. Just for the two of them. But their reality was not the reality that their companions were experiencing.

The moment Nora had responded to the kiss, the cracks had suddenly started shrinking until they completely disappeared. And then, when they were all gone from the walls, the rocks that had surrounded them for as long as they had been inside the cave, vanished. Just like that: gone for good.

'Congratulations, you have achieved what we tried to achieve but failed so long ago,' said a woman's voice. It sounded familiar to them all, but it was not until the person who had talked walked out of the forest, that they could stop shaking all along. The amazement at their sight, however, made them all lose their speech. Thus, after a few awkward minutes, the woman continued talking: 'Nora Elisabeth, Gabriel Aksel, your pure, true love has lifted the enchantment that has laid over this forest for as long as we can remember. Nobody really knows when the curse was cast, or what for, but the truth is we have lived our whole lives trying to get rid of it.

»We understand everything you have gone through. We have felt the same anger, hopelessness, fear, and whatever else you have felt. We dealt with the same issues when we were kids. And even though we did not succeed back then, we have now. Neither of us understood it back then, but time has taught us that each of us is meant for greatness at a different time in our lives. We felt empty and disappointed with ourselves, but that was because we did not fully understand the situation. Mankind has evolved because each generation has learned from their previous ones. And that's what we did. We were never meant to get rid of this curse ourselves, but to guide you towards doing it,' said Mary. She, together with her fellow friends, had kept walking towards what had been the centre of the cave. They were now face to face with their grandkids.

'Mary? Is that you?' asked Cynthia when she recomposed.

'Indeed,' said Mary, holding her tears.

'Do you know each other?' said Mark, astonished.

'Of course, I do. She is my sister,' said Mary, as though that was the most obvious thing to say. She then walked towards an emotional Cynthia as fast as her elder legs allowed her to, and embraced her very tightly. They had been apart for decades, and even though they were not the same persons they knew, a sibling is a sibling for life. 'When your grandma and I pursued the legend, we could not get rid of the enchantment, and thus had to leave someone behind. We of course tried to bypass that necessity, but what is meant to be, is meant to be. I wonder, however,... how did you do it? We walked all the way inside the cave, but at a certain point, we couldn't walk any further. I remember a very odd voice in my head, a voice that didn't seem to say anything at all. And then, we were outside, feeling very sleepy'.

'Nora did it,' said Theresa. She dared to talk for her friend, who was all shocked and reddened. 'Her pendant wasn't just a pendant, but a sort of amulet as well. From the very beginning, she was able to understand what was being said. Because, as difficult as it might be for you to understand, that noise you remember wasn't but the actual instructions to leave. They just needed to be heard by the right person,' added Theresa, turning from Mary and Cynthia to her brother and Nora.

'I see...,' said a thoughtful Mary. 'I'm glad it's over now though. I've got a lot of to catch up with this little one' she added, wiping up her sister's cheeks. Once done, she looked up at Nora and added: 'and you must get ready to leave to London. Your parents will be here any minute'.

'What do you mean my parents will be here any minute?' said Nora, letting go of Gabe. 'It was only yesterday they left to Glasgow'.

'Time was frozen inside the cave. You haven't aged a single minute since you entered it. However, because you were inside for a very short time, you can't tell on your selves. But look at them. My sister is my age, yet she looks like a teenager,' said Mary, standing up and helping her sister do the same. 'Enough with the chit chat anyway. We really need to get going'.

And, as soon as she finished talking, she turned around and started walking her way out of The Enchanted Forest. She did not look back a single time to see whether she was being followed by the others, because she trusted they would. Beyond her, the worst thing one can make to instil confidence in others is to force them to do something against their will. Some people might understand the circumstances the minute they happen, and others might need minutes, hours, or even years. Regardless of the time required to do so, however, we all end up finding the truth within ourselves.

Epilogue

Eileen finished packing her clothes just the minute her alarm went off. She had had a very light sleep that night and thus had woken up the moment the light had filtered in between the curtains. She turned it off, put on her slippers and head downstairs to have the last breakfast of that summer with her grandparents.

'Mo'ning!' said Alick the moment Eileen entered the kitchen. 'Toasts?' he asked, lifting the bread bag he had on his hands.

'Please,' was all Eileen said for a reply. After that, she opened the cutlery cupboard and asked whether her grandmother had already had her breakfast. But before Alick was able to say anything, she saw her grandmother sitting on the bench in the backyard. She had been on such a rollercoaster of emotions ever since they had talked to Klara Herrmann, that neither Eileen nor her grandfather knew what they could do to help her. And thus they had decided to leave her at her own pace.

'She'll get ove' it… eventually,' said Alick, sitting at the dining table. 'Changing topics howeve'... what a maste'piece ye've created! I luv it. I ab-so-lu-te-ly luv it. When ye sta'ted rewriting it, did ye know ye would end it like ye did?'.

'Not really. I allowed the circumstances of the moment to determine the path. To be honest, when writing a story it is easier to take things that have happened to you, or that you have heard that have happened to somebody else, and rearrange them so they fit into your scheme. That way, it is much easier to make the story look real, even when it's fantasy you are talking about. You can give a good bunch of detail to make the feeling leave the page and embrace the reader,' said Eileen, sitting down at the dining table.

'Fair enough. And… I'm curious. When ye first wrote the story, did ye know how to end it?'.

'Actually, I did and I didn't at the same time,' said Eileen, giggling. 'I know it might sound weird to you, but we authors never really stop having ideas. And yes, I counted myself as an author' she added, pointing at herself with both her hands and smiling widely. 'It's the means of reaching the end that might actually give us some trouble, but I enjoy writing. And that's the only reason why I do it. As a teenager, I never let people read my stories until they were finished, but back then they were not that long. It is the process of creation that matters anyway. It has its ups and downs, but once you have the finished product in your hands, you only seem to remember the good moments'.

'And what we'e those?'.

'Well… to start with, once I typed the last letter, I felt really proud of myself. I had once dreamed of writing a novel, and I did eventually! Whether it is the first one of tons of them, only time will tell. But having wandered the journey has taught me so much, that I think I am a different person now'.

'Well, ye have discovered things of yerself that ye didn't know befo'ehand, and I'm not just talking 'bout yer capability to finish a novel'.

'You know what? I guess the Klara-Clarissa thing only added a push inside of me. I now know how much it meant for grandma, and how difficult it might have been to deal with that her whole life. I have never met my parents, but I wanted to tribute them and let grandma know that we all deal with our own battles. We both have experienced that talking is the easiest solution to our problems. We share the capability of speech for a reason'.

'And did ye ever allow ye to surprise yerself during the process?'.

'Constantly!' exclaimed Eileen amongst laughs. Her grandfather had proved to be a much more enquiring interlocutor than she had expected he would be. 'I told you when I arrived here that I had a completely different mindset for the summer. I was planning on writing something from scratch, but I ended up rewriting my former story. And don't take me wrong, I'm not disappointed with the result at all. I guess I'll just let destiny do its job, if that exists at all'.

'Fair enough. Although don't get too comfortable. This old man needs more stories,' added Alick before swallowing the last bit of toast he had left.

ACKNOWLEDGEMENTS

I would like to thank

Ainara E., for being the guinea pig of my cliff-hangers. She patiently waited for my chapters to be delivered, knowing that she would have to wait for days (when not weeks) until the following chapter. Her screenshots and comments about the plot have helped writing this story more than she thinks.

Christina B., for her critical eye. She also read part of the manuscript before it was finished and suggested changes that I had not thought about, but that truly added a different dimension to the story. I am so glad she found out what I needed without telling her.

Till, der Mann mit dem durchsichtigen Regenmantel. Vielen Dank, dass du mir mit den deutsche Sätzen geholfen hast. Ich muss nicht bekannt sein, um mich bei dir für deine Hilfe zu bedanken.

My housemate, Clara C., for her patience with me running in the house during the COVID-19 lockdown. Or when I turned the kitchen into a bakery. Creating a novel takes time and requires escape routes that could be annoying for those around. Destiny brought us together because we are as clumsy, and thank goodness it did!

My mum, Eva, for buying me my first Harry Potter book. Like a good millennial, that saga changed my life forever. Even though when I started writing I could not get past 15 pages,

I never despaired because I wanted to, someday, be able to write a vibrating story as JK Rowling had.

My dad, Juan Carlos, for instilling in me the culture of sports. Most people will only see how you perform on the due day but will be completely unaware of the efforts you made during practice. Yet a bad match does not define who you are. Only practice can take you to glory.

My brother, Adrián, for playing with me when we were kids. We were the masters back then; we made up the rules.

The rest of my family, for being there. One cannot choose their family, but if I had had the chance, I would have not chosen anybody else.

And to you. You deserve a big round of applause if you have reached this page.

ABOUT THE AUTHOR

GIOVANNA DE LA HOZ (Navarre, Spain 1995) has a BSc in Biology and an MSc in Drug Development, both by the University of Salamanca. She currently works in the Process Development Department of a biotechnology company. She has been fond of writing ever since she was a teenager, and this is her debut novel! She wrote most of this story during the 2020 COVID-19 lockdown.

Ptss, it is Giovanna here. Well, not that it has not been me for the whole book hehe anyways, I am writing these lines because I would like you to know that I have created an email account to hear from you! I would be more than thrilled to read whatever you have got to say.

So please, do drop me a few lines at the6thsymphony@gmail.com. I speak a bunch of languages (namely Spanish, English, French, Catalan and German), and understand a decent amount of Portuguese and Italian, so feel free to contact me in any of them.

¡Gracias!	Danke!
Thank you!	Obrigada!
Merci!	Grazie!
Graciès!	

And in case you were wondering, the photo that I chose was not coincidental. Is English my mother tongue? No, it is not. Did I manage to write a full-length novel in English? Yes, I did. Are there mistakes? I would be surprised if there were not any, to be honest. But it is my perfectly imperfect debut novel so I guess I can say *Ops, I did it!*